SCARY STORIES
IN THE DARK:

scary tales collection. horror short stories for kids, teens and adults of all ages (Vol 1-2-3)

Table of content

INTRODUCTION

Do you love horror stories? The type of stories that you read to your children to warn them about the horrors of the night? Are you a newcomer to the genre, or are you a veteran that has already went through the raunchiest most devastating stories out there already? Well then, this is the perfect midnight "snack" for you.

This anthology story depicts every corner of hell possible in order to make you feel that chill running down your spine. Whether it's ghosts, killers, monsters or whatnot, we've got you covered. These stories are also for all ages, although we will say that we're not afraid to get into the gory details either.

So, are you interested in a thrilling mystery? Will the detective find the right answers before it all goes to "hell", or will he fail, missing the trail of bodies altogether? Will the cute foreign couple take the mental abuse from their boss lying down or will they fight back, one slice at a time? Is that your wife sitting next to your bed or is it something else?

Who knows, really? After all, this is horror, it doesn't need a happy ending to end, it only needs an "end". So, if this sounds like a blast for you and your children then give it a try. It's perfect to spook your children, but at the same time it can make grown adults shiver in their trousers too.

It's like a wise man once said, "You can't make an omelet without breaking a few skulls". And oh boy, this book sure delivers on this promise.

So, just sit back, get yourself a hot cup of coffee and get ready, because this ride is getting bumpier and bumpier with every story. The destination of this carousel of horrors? That depends, have you been a good person?

SCARY STORIES: VOL.1

STORY N.1: FACELESS WIND

"Mason, Andrew, Michael and Simon were in the attic arguing about superhero characters after they had just played an enthralling round of Dungeons and Dragons.

"I think we should play scrabble next" Michael, who was their host, said.

Michael lived with his parents in a house just overlooking the woods. It was his first time hosting his friends in his house. Not many people came around that part of town.

"Why scrabble though?" Andrew asked. "Let's keep playing Dungeons and Dragons".

"I want scrabble! I want to see words take forms. I have learned new words; like gnomes and hoax. I want to eat you raw, as usual" Michael said, cackling like a duck. The other boys laughed too, except for Simon.

Simon had been skeptical about the whole visit. His parents didn't like Michael's family. His mother, especially. She was envious of the never-aging skin of Michael's mother. The skepticism spread to him, too. So, when she had hugged them upon their arrival, he tried as much as he could to break free from the tight and surprisingly bony hug. He could feel her ribs poking at him and a strange hollow in the area where her belly should be. He was scared to the teeth. His fears got even worse when he found Michael's father looking at him from the window when they were playing a game of ball in the afternoon. But he said nothing. Maybe, he was over-thinking the whole thing, he thought.

It didn't seem any more like over-thinking though, when they were having dinner. Michael's parents crunched their meat with a ravenousness he had never seen and they talked smoothly over the table. The whole time, it never seemed like their mouths weren't moving. His other friends just dug at their plates and chattered like weaverbirds.

"Don't you like the...meat?" Michael's father asked Simon.

"Why, yes I do!" Simon replied, nervously and his friends turned to look at him.

"Eat up, son. Fatten up". Simon shifted uncomfortably in his chair and nodded; the man had his gaze fixed on him.

Maybe they are vampires, Simon thought. That would have explained the slow aging of Michael's mother. Who knows?

"Maybe you need some water to down the meat? I know it's a bit springy but it's the best"

Simon nodded and flushed the meat down his throat without chewing.

As they set up the scrabble board, the attic window startled to rattle; softly.

"That rattling is distracting me. Go fasten the latch, Simon" Michael said.

Simon walked to the window with wobbly legs and fastened it but, in the process, he looked down at the vast woods that almost encircled the house. He could see a small piece of light venturing farther into the woods and thinning and thinning. Just then, a crow smashed into the glass window and slid down.

"Dammit!" Simon screamed.

His friends scurried to his side and ask what made the racket.

"Look," Simon said. "A crow smashed into the glass. How many times do you see that?"

There was a small trail of blood on the glass. Michael decided to go down and go check on the fallen bird.

"Keep at the game. We will be together soon" He said, going out.

Everything about the statement was wrong to Simon. Why not just say 'I will be back soon', Simon pondered.

"Hey, Simon. You have been awfully quiet today" Andrew said, punching him on his arm.

Simon gave him a smile and just said he was feeling drowsy.

"Me too. Especially after eating that meat. That was more springy than any other meat I have ever had" Mason said, dully.

"Yes, Michael's dad said it was fresh meat. Very tasty, right?" Andrew chirped.

"Fresh meat? Definitely not beef"

"Yes. He said it is..." Andrew had barely completed his statement when the attic window started to rattle again; this time, louder.

Simon turned sharply to look at the window and he could have sworn that he saw someone. The face disappeared as soon he turned. Goosebumps popped on his arms. He had a feeling that he was being watched. He couldn't shake the thought off.

"Strange, right? I thought I saw something" Simon said. Nobody said anything.

The light flickered off for a moment and then came back on.

"What's up with the power?" Andrew said. "Let me go check on Michael"

Andrew ran downstairs from the attic leaving Simon and Mason to play the game. The both of them were too shaken to play though. They didn't say anything to each other. They just waited.

Minutes stretched and both Michael and Andrew were still not back.

"What's going on down there?" Mason asked - his voice shaky. The light went off again. This time, it flickered on and off.

"I don't know—" Simon said and walked to the stairs. "Michael?! Andrew?! What's taking you both so long?"

His voice wafted down like he was shouting into a hollow tube.

No reply.

When the lights came back on, Mason drew out a toolbox from underneath the table and picked the flashlights.

"Let's go see for ourselves" he said, handing one of the flashlights to Simon.

They walked gently down the wooden stairs. But the wood creaked under their feet.

There was no sign of Andrew, Michael or even his parents.

The door started to rattle violently too. For a month, they both feared it would fly open and break free from the hinges. As the rattling quietened, the light went off again. Simon heard Mason's torch drop on the floor and when he flashed his light on, Mason was nowhere to be seen. Simon shrieked.

"Mason!" he cried, moving backwards towards the door and his back struck a sturdy figure, he turned around slowly and the man he saw had no eyes or mouth or stomach - only the blonde hair of Michael's father. He bolted to the door, which was now tightly shut and tried to force it open. Just as the man's crow-like fingers circled around his neck, the door open and he fell out. He ran. And ran. And ran into the woods, screaming for help. Behind him was a swift sweeping sound chasing. The woods stretched and stretched and the boy thinned and thinned until he became like wind" "

The boys were visibly shaken now and they huddled close to themselves.

"Did the thing get him?" one of the boys asked Jerry, the storyteller.

"No. But he became faceless too. He lives in the wind now. His cries are its howls. He comes when you invite him, though"

"Who would want to do that?"

"You invite him by telling his story. I think we already did"

The winds howled and the curtains swayed like they had been embodied. Jerry switched off the lights and laughed.

"Turn the lights back on. That's not funny"

Jerry turned it back on and the howling stopped. But Jerry was nowhere to be seen. Where the curtain once was, a faceless man stood.

STORY N.2: GHOST HOUSE

George woke up with big plans today. It was his second week in the neighborhood and he had prepared to go check the haunted house his neighbors talked about. It was a crappy story. They said the people who lived there mysteriously died in their sleep one night and nobody knew until a week later when their remains were found rotten.

"They had always been strange, you know?" Matt, his neighbor, said after narrating the story.

"Surprising!"

"More like creepy. Their bodies were found on the couch facing the TV. Almost liked they died watching it" Matt said, with a half-smile. "That's kinda like the way I'd love to die"

"How? Alone and forgotten?"

"No. Die watching TV - maybe even watching SpongeBob. That would be the classiest way to die"

George shook his head and chuckled. At least, he had one friend in Arizona who had a dark sense of humor.

"So, are you going to come with me?" George asked.

"Nope. Nothing new there to see"

George shrugged.

So that morning, George woke up, wore his favorite jean and set out. The lawn of the supposedly haunted house was surprisingly mowed.

"Hello?!" his voice echoed back at him in manifolds.

He smiled to himself and continued snooping around. First, he went to the master bedroom that had massive wardrobes, then to the kids' rooms - one of them had a worn out poster of Madonna nailed to the wall and a picture of the family smiling - then to the kitchen. The tables were neat - in fact, very neat. When he rubbed his thumb over the table, there was not a single speck of dust on it. Who could have been maintaining such a place for this long, he wondered. He took pictures of the kitchen and even slipped a fork into his pocket for keepsake.

Confident and happy with his adventure, he decided to wander to the basement. It was the only dusty part of the house.

Suddenly, he heard the front door open. A flurry of voices followed; voices of children and that of their parents cautioning them against running in the sitting room.

"Meredith, that's my doll. Give it back!" one of the girls said.

Meredith? Now, he was alarmed. Meredith was the name of one of the girls that died in this house.

"No, Jenny. C'mon! Yours is in the basement, remember?" the other replied.

George froze. Those were the girls that died years ago. And now, she wants to come to the basement? He heard the footsteps approach the basement. She climbed down the steps and, with a flashlight, she searched for her doll. George hid in the darkest corner of the basement.

She dusted the brown, dirty doll when she found it and made to climb back up. He was going to heave a heavy a sigh of relief when she turned swiftly and flashed the light in his direction. George could feel himself dying under the light. He waited for her to gasp and call for the other ghosts to come but she didn't. She flashed the light at some other place and left. His heart slid down his throat. When he realized he couldn't be seen, he climbed up.

The ghost family went about their business oblivious of his existence. George took pictures of them; pleased with his big find.

"Dad, come see this. The president is making an announcement" Meredith called out.

"Gimme a sec, dear".

George turned to look at the TV which wasn't there when he first walked in and on the screen, the president there was Barrack Obama. How could it be? Times have changed. The father sat on the couch and groaned. He dropped a newspaper that had been under his arms onto the table. The paper read July 20, 2010 which was the year the entire family died.

"Honey!" the wife called from the kitchen.

"Now, what is it again?" he said, exhaustion evident in his voice.

The wife came in with the youngest daughter rushing behind her like a mean cat.

"I can't find my fork!" she yelled. "Someone musta' took it"

George froze again.

"Yes, someone musta' took it. I know this. Someone was 'ere. I know it. I know it" she repeated, stomping her feet like she stood on a colony of soldier ants.

"Calm down, little, bad bear. We'll find it. Let Daddy watch the news" her dad said, his eyes darting across the room.

"Come, Betty. I will get you another one. Tut-tut. Say no more" the mom said, rubbing her short, curly hair.

After the fork issue, the house was quiet. For inexplicable reason, George couldn't get himself to leave the room. He was transfixed.

"Okay, babies. Time for lunch" the mother announced, coming with a tray filled with small porcelain dishes. Steam danced out of the plates and filled the room. The aroma tickled George's nostrils. It was sharp and bitter. George's hand flew straight to his nose and he tried to stifle the cough that was raging to burst from his throat.

They sat at their dining and ate with grave silence, the clink of their plates were the only sounds.

"Gee, I dunno. My room smells different" Danny, the boy, said.

"I know, I know" the father said, wiping the soup that slipped from his mouth.

When they finished their dinner, they all sat at the long couch in the same way they had been pictured sitting when they died. They were still for minutes. Once in a while, they would sigh and exchange grave looks.

"Danny, draw the drapes" the father instructed, huskily.

The room became dim and only the light from the TV illuminated the room. They were watching the TV with great concentration.

"It's that time of the year again..." the father began.

"It's that time of the year again..." they chorused, solemnly.

George narrowed his eyes at them. Suddenly, his phone alarm rang. He had set it for 5pm.

"Oh no, oh no" he muttered under his breath. The ghosts had heard his phone ring. They looked back sharply, but not directly because they couldn't see him. The father stood up and sniffed. He walked close to the area where George stood like a pole; holding his breath like a boy learning to swim. The man sniffed deeper and soon, he was face-to-face with George but he couldn't see. He poked his finger at George and it passed through his body like light. Seeing that man close-up, George noticed how pale he looked; so pale he was almost translucent.

His children and wife looked at him keenly. When he nodded his head, Danny reached for the TV remote and switched the station. A video of George started to play; a video of all he had done since he entered the house. It started with him stealing a fork from the kitchen (to which the aggrieved girl shouted "I told you someone took it"), and him in the basement. It was almost like someone followed him with a camera all through. The idea made his hair stand on his neck like the spikes on a porcupine.

They hit the forward button until they got to the present. George was looking at himself on the TV standing right behind the family seated on the couch and they all turned backwards!

This time, George could feel the directness of their gaze. They had seen him! They all stood up at once. George shrieked like a banshee and flew up the stairs into the master bedroom. He dived into the wardrobe and shut it close. He placed his hand over his pounding chest. An eye peeped at him through the wardrobe's keyhole. He screamed and, with the fork in his pocket, thrust at it. Immediately, the eye vanished. After staying there for minutes, crying and trying to steady himself, he opened the wardrobe. Lo, the previously neat house had devolved into an abandoned building. It looked as spooky as can be and worse, he realized he had been hiding in a box. When he looked at his hand, he wasn't holding a fork but a crow's foot.

He dropped it as though it were red-hot iron and wiped his hand on his dirty trouser. The cobwebs clung stubbornly to his hair and cloth. He zoomed off; the sitting room where he had, only minutes ago, stood was in worse shape. The chandeliers dangled and looked like it would drop any minute. He pushed the door and bolted out of the lawn. The lawn was filled with dry leaves and there was a crunch in every step he took in his galloping run. By the time he reached down the street, he was huffing and puffing like a boxer after the eleventh round.

He showed down when he reached his house because his parents' cars weren't parked in the driveway and there was no way he was going to stay in the house alone. Just then, he felt a warm hand tap him. He nearly screamed again but he saw it was just Matt.

"Hey! Look who we have here, Spiderman!" Matt laughed. "What's this you got all over your hair?"

"Dude..." George said, swallowing hard. "That house is haunted"

"Come on, I was only joking. It's not haunted, it's just an abandoned property" Matt replied, waving his hand as if he was dispelling a bad smell.

"Maybe you were. But it's haunted! I am serious. I was there"

"People are there every weekend. Middle-school kids go there to play hide-and-seek"

George remembered he took photos of the house so he whipped out his phone and wiped the screen.

"Look –" he said, as he searched through his gallery. He clicked on one of the pictures and it opened with a message "Unsupported file format".

"Yes? What am I supposed to see?" Matt said, mockingly.

"Ghosts, whatever!"

"I didn't see anything. Are you even listening to yourself? You need sleep".

George ate his dinner quietly and went to his room. He dismissed all the ideas of ghost as just imaginations. He rolled onto his bed and, for the second time, checked his phone's gallery. This time, the pictures opened. But it wasn't a picture he took earlier. It was a picture of the ghost father watching him from his own window - and grinning. A chill rushed through his body and a shadow loomed over him.

STORY N.3: RED-EYED SNOW

Little Johnny had a cute, white cat named Snow. It was lovely and everyone who ever saw the cat wanted to hold it and stroke it. And when they did, it would purr sweetly. He had found the cat one evening on his way home and, seeing how beautiful and lonely it was, took it home. His mother, Mrs. Byers, didn't care so much for the cat. She always said she hated how the cat looked at her but she let him keep it anyway. After Johnny's father died, he had become recluse and quiet but that evening, she saw the sparkle return to her son's eyes. They became inseparable.

But for school policies, he would have loved to take the cat to his class too. His eyes would always pool whenever he had to leave for school. Snow would sit at the door and stare sadly at him.

"You just hang in there, buddy. I will be right back" Johnny would always say.

One day, Johnny and his friends had to go for an excursion that would keep him away from Snow for two days. He had no choice but to leave the cat in his mother's hands. "Mom, it's just two days -"

"Why can't you just take it with you?"

"They said 'No Pets' " Johnny said, rubbing Snow's body.

Sensing Johnny's sadness, Snow had curled up on Johnny's laps.

"OK!"

"All you have to do is give it milk - put it in the pink bowl - it's his favorite" Johnny said, and added, "You can stroke it at night, too. He loves that"

"Johnny, you are reaching -" His mom cautioned.

"C'mon mom, Snow is a good, good cat" Johnny said, pouting. "Right, Snow?"

Snow looked from mother to son, and from son to mother. It meowed and looked away.

"There's no way that cat is getting on my bed. I will give it milk and no more" His mother said.

When Johnny turned to wave at Snow before he jumped on the school bus, he saw that Snow wasn't looking at him. Snow knew that Johnny would be gone for a while. It felt it, somehow.

"Be safe, baby" Johnny's mother called at Johnny and waved from the door before shutting it close.

Everything went fine during the day. Snow was soft and lovely as usual and he quickly lapped up the milk he was fed.

"This is much easier than I had expected" the mother thought, casting a glance at the silent cat.

"Time for bed now, OK? Up you go" she announced as though the cat could hear her. Snow climbed up the stairs and entered Johnny's room.

Deep into the night, Johnny's mother started to hear train sounds from her son's room. At first, she thought the sounds were in her head. But when it continued, she groggily got off her bed and checked the room. Her son's toy train was running round the track and its red and blue lights rotated and colored the dark room like a sinister club house.

Snow crouched in front of the train and watched it go in circles.

"What's happening here?" she asked, her voice shaky. Who could have powered the train, she wondered. There was no way a cat could have done that.

Snow looked at her sharply and sprawled on the floor on its belly.

That look shot fear into the back of her knee. She assumed she was just assuming things but didn't she just catch a glint of red in Snow's eye or was it the light from the train? With great effort, she disconnected the train and shooed the cat with her feet. It meowed - something about the meow was unnatural. It sounded almost like a growl.

She hurried out of the room and although, she forced herself to sleep, she couldn't.

Things proceeded well the next morning but Mrs. Byers couldn't help but notice the cat's hyperactivity. It ran up and down the stairs as though it were in a game of chase. When Mrs. Byers couldn't handle the situation any longer, she locked the door and left her house.

***

Upon return, she found the cat by the door gnarling like a hungry beast. It was then she realized that she hadn't fed it the whole day.

"Oh dear..." she said, slapping her forehead. "I am so sorry. I will fix you..." she stopped in her track when she saw the mess in the sitting room. The cat had ripped out Johnny's favorite teddy-bear to shreds. The head had been bitten off, the eyes too and scattered everywhere, were the pieces of its brown coat and yellow foam.

She turned to scold the cat but it had crouched dangerously as if planning an offensive.

She wondered if she needed to call a vet to come check the cat up or if the cat was just possessed.

"No, possessed cats exist only in movies" she reassured herself.

One more night, she said. One more night and Johnny would be back and they would kick this cat out of the house.

That night she was awoken by the loud sound from the TV. She walked down the stairs in half-sleep and in the living room was Snow watching a television she was damn sure she had switched off before going to bed. And he was standing on his hind legs; on twos. Its eyes were flaming red now. She was sure about it.

***

When Johnny returned, he flew straight into the house, ignoring his mother who was standing at the porch; arms spread. The cat licked his face and he laughed; tickled by the warmth.

"Hey, mom. Did you take care of this cute, little thing?"

"Yes, and about the cat, we need to talk!"

"Mom, later. Please. There are many stories I need to tell Snow"

"Johnny-" but he was already on his way up the stairs.

After dinner however, she dragged him to the kitchen whilst Snow curled on the couch.

"Something is off about your cat"

"What? You didn't even bond with my cat while I was away. He must have been so lonely"

"Listen, your cat does things"

"What things?"

"I saw it stand on its hind legs, it connected your train, it turned the TV on. Have you seen its eyes at night?"

"Mom, are you making this up?"

"What, no!" she said, then in a hushed tone, she said, "Have you seen your teddy?"

Johnny nodded in the negative.

"It tore your teddy to shreds"

"Maybe you didn't feed it enough"

"Trust me; you haven't seen things I have seen..."

Johnny didn't believe any of this, though.

"So you want me to throw Snow out?"

Of course, she wanted that. The cat had gone wild. Who knew what else he would devour? But she shook her head and said no.

"We'll take it to a vet" she said with a smile.

***

She had hoped the vet would find something wrong with him but he said the cat was fine and, as he added, in perfect condition. Johnny was overjoyed. He stroked Snow's body all through their quiet drive home. But luck would later shine on Mrs. Byers.

On a sweltering Saturday afternoon, someone knocked on their door.

"Hello" Mrs. Byers said to the thin boy who had knocked.

"Hello..." he replied, his voice was as thin as he was. "Is this the Byers'?"

The boy's eyes had sunken in and his thin shirt matted to his skin. Mrs. Byers could make out the outline of his ribs.

"Yes"

"I am looking for my cat. This -" he said, holding up a picture of Snow and himself. "Some folks said they saw it 'round here"

"Johnny, come down here!" Mrs. Byers called. "Someone's looking for Snow"

Johnny stared at the boy like an angry hen watching a hawk swoop down on her chick.

He looked at the picture the boy showed him. It was clearly Snow and it was taken a year ago, as the timeline in the picture indicated. That was before Johnny found the cat.

"But I really love Snow" Johnny said, defeated. "I love Sn... I love my cat, too" the boy replied coldly and swatted at a fly that buzzed close to his ear.

"Then, where have you been all this while?"

"Away"

"Did you even care what happened to him?"

"Yes. It's why I have come find him"

"You stay nearby?"

"Yes, at 23. Old Downing"

When Snow sighted the boy at the door, it galloped into his thin arms and the boy cradled it. That was the last straw that broke Johnny.

"Mom, are you going to say anything?"

"I will get you another cat, dear"

***

Days passed and Johnny couldn't bear the loss anymore so he resolved to go check on Snow and plead with the boy to have him back for a week.

He found the house easily; two men sat out front. He assumed they were the boy's parents.

"Hello, sirs"

"Hello, boy"

"Please, I am looking for a Jimmy"

"Jimmy?" they asked in unison.

"Yes, the one with the cat?"

The men exchanged looks.

"Are you his friend?"

"Yes?"

"Doubt that!"

"Why?"

"If you were his friend, you'd know he died a year ago. His parents sold the house and moved on to Metro"

Johnny was speechless and surprised. The men took pity on him.

"Would you like some water, kid?"

"No, thanks. What about his cat?"

"The evil, white cat? They sold it, too. They couldn't bear its trouble anymore. One time, the cat was at the cemetery trying to unearth a freshly buried person"

"Last I heard of him, he ate two full hens from Nana's backyard" the other man chipped in.

"Aye, that cat. It doesn't leave your home until it draws some blood"

Blood? Lots of wild thoughts rushed into Johnny's head. He nearly puked knowing that he had allowed the cat lick his face many times in the past. He thanked the men and cycled home as fast as he could.

STORY N.4: MISS FAIRBORN'S AUCTION

When Mason looked at his bathroom mirror, he was there again. It was a face he had now mastered - only this time, the eyes were redder. Like tomatoes. The boy smiled; not a friendly smile but one laced with anger. In a fit of fear, Mason screamed and punched the mirror. His mom was first to rush into the bathroom to check. They didn't understand, at first, the history between Mason and the boy, whose had now broken in the cracked mirror and vanished. Theirs was a story that started on the night after the auction. Sometimes it seemed like the universe forcefully arranged for people to meet; its force so strong that nothing could change.

There was no uncle Mason loved as much as he loved Uncle Sylvester. So it was a thing of joy when his parents announced that they would be spending the holidays over at his place in Manhattan. But two days to the visit, his parents changed their mind. They were going to spend it in Ibiza instead. His mom was nuts over getting a tan. Mason couldn't count how many times he had spent his holiday at that particular beach with his parents. In the beginning, he used to like those holidays but it had since lost its appeal to him.

"No, I don't want to go to the beach this year" he complained, bitterly.

"Well, it doesn't look like you've got much of a choice" his dad replied, his mouth full with salad.

Mason fumed and looked at his mom.

"Mom? Are you going to come in on this?"

"I am sorry, son. Your dad and I really need this trip. Right, honey?" she replied, winking at her husband and placing a hand on his knee. Mason's father chuckled and said, of course.

"Well, I can go by myself to Uncle Sylvester's" Mason said, determined to force their hand.

"That's the problem. Your uncle is busy these days, you know, going to auctions and doing his thing. Besides, the beach isn't such a bad idea. You get to surf on those waves you love"

"Auctions? I would love that!"

"You are going to choose auctions over surfing?"

Mason thought over this for a while. It was a trick question and his father knew he had him against the ropes. Truthfully, he would rather go surfing than go to an auction but he would also prefer to meet Uncle Sylvester than to go surfing. So he said, yes, auctions over surfing a hundred times over.

His father eyed him in surprise and laughed. Mason knew that laugh; he had won. His father ringed Uncle Sylvester and two days later, Mason arrived at his place.

"Wow. 15 and you already look this big!" Uncle Sylvester remarked, covering him in a bear hug. They talked all evening and Mason went to bed to rest. "You'll need all the strength you can get tomorrow"

"Is it going to be fun?" Mason asked.

"Sure. There's going to be a bubbling crowd. Miss Fairborn was quite popular. Lots of people are going to want to have their hands on her antiques"

"Doesn't she have children to inherit them all?"

"None that I know of. None that is alive, I mean to say"

Mason was thrilled. He slept with a wide grin plastered on his face.

***

True to Uncle Sylvester's words, a buzzing crowd had gathered in front of the Fairborn mansion that was only a stone's throw from Uncle Sylvester's house. An auctioneer with a funny, red hat stood atop a raised platform and rambled in a way that amused Mason.

"Four, four, who will gimme fourna quatta, quattava dollar?" he said, advertising a mug. He wiped his sweaty brows and looked at the bargaining crowd.

"Five? Do I hear six? Six! Gone to the man in blue!" he said, passing the mug to a young boy by his side to package.

"Wow, this is cool!" Mason laughed.

They moved away from the crowd and walked around the place, picking up items and inspecting them.

"Look at this –" Mason said, holding up a small alarm clock to his uncle.

"You like it?"

"Well, it's nice..."

"Then, we should get it. I will take it up to the auctioneer. Anything else?"

"This mirror, too. I love the patterns"

It appeared the two items were the least bid for. The auctioneer announced and strangely, nobody else wanted it. A triumphant Mason took his new possessions to the house and they nailed the mirror to the wall. Uncle Sylvester complimented it too. It was just adjacent to the window and it caught the golden light of the setting sun. From the window of the guest room he was assigned, he watched as the crowd slowly dispersed from the grounds of the Fairborn mansion.

He set his new alarm clock for 7am and slept off happily after phoning his parents. Once his alarm rang, he ran into the bathroom and brushed his teeth. As he wiped the towel over his face, he became aware of the time of the day. It was still quiet and dark!

"What in God's name –" he muttered, and ran to the window. A soft breeze caressed his face as he opened the window. The street was quiet and only two faint lights appeared on the street;

one from the Bed-n-Breakfast downtown and the other was a dull, moving light from the Fairborn mansion. He was a bit surprised that anyone would still be within the premises at that time but was more surprised at the falseness of his alarm. He slid back onto his bed and reset it.

The next morning, he explained what happened to his uncle who laughed at the whole thing.

"Some of these antiques are best for decoration. Most are already too old and you know how cranked up old things are"

"I know. But I clearly remember setting it at 7am and not 12am"

"Well, old stuff" his uncle shrugged and gulped down his coffee.

But this did not stop! That night, the alarm had sounded at the same time - 12am! Mason was a bit scared now. He sat on his bed and inspected the clock. For the first time, he noticed an inscription on it. The initials "A.F" were etched onto its side. He shook the clock and listened for any broken part - nothing!

He didn't tell his uncle about its continuity. This continued for two more nights. On one of those nights, the alarm had sounded and Mason sleepwalked down the stairs and only stood when his head heavily hit the mahogany door. It was at this point he decided that he was going to unravel the mystery of the clock.

When he went to bed the next night, he lay facing the clock and kept his eyes open. As the clock neared 12am, he felt an atmospheric shift in the room - the same way you'd feel when you turned the air conditioner on. Mason narrowed his eyes and to his horror, a boy dressed in a neat school uniform appeared from the walls. A cloud of blue-white light surrounded him. For a while, he stood, after which he floated to the mirror they had gotten from the auction and combed his hair with a small comb he produced from his breast pocket. He parted his already-oiled hair at the sides and floated to Mason's bedside. Mason said a short but heartfelt prayer, hoping the boy doesn't look at his eyes - he knew his eyeballs were running left and right under his eyelids like someone having a nightmare.

The boy reset the clock a couple of clicks back and waited. Mason wondered if he could hear his drumming heart or his unsteady breathing but even if he did, he showed no sign of it. In what seemed like hours (it was actually only a couple of minutes), the hour hand struck 12 and the alarm buzzed. The light surrounding the boy suddenly dimmed and the boy walked right through the walls away from the room. Mason opened his eyes fully and looked around. A cold sweat had broken on his body like a person down with fever. He immediately opened his window and like the previous night, he saw the dim light moving around in the old and dark Fairborn house.

He kept this incident from his uncle and resolved to find out more. He casually asked about the dead son of Miss Fairborn during a conversation with his uncle in the afternoon.

"His name was Alfred, I think. Why?"

"Curious!"

"Don't tell me you've caught the Fairborn fever"

"The what?"

His uncle chuckled and said, "You know, it's a fascinating family. I was just as curious about them as you are now when I first came here"

"I see" Mason said. It clicked now. The initials on the clock meant Alfred Fairborn. The mirror and clock were his. But what would the ghost of Alfred doing floating around in his school uniform?

The boy repeated the same routine the following night. This time, as he sat by the bedside, he kept muttering, "I won't be late. I won't be late. I won't be late". At the strike of 12, he vanished again.

When night came the next day, Mason held the mirror the same way he'd seen the boy hold it and waited. He felt the hair on his neck stand on its end when the boy came, he was looking right at the boy from the mirror. The boy watched him and for the first time, he saw the gash on his head. Blood dripped from his head onto his uniform. The boy fixed his cold gaze at him and then his face went soft. He floated to Mason and softly, he whispered, "Come!"

He didn't wait for Mason. He started to float away; not through the walls this time but the stairs. Mason followed behind but the boy was fast. At every turn, he'd turn around and beckon on Mason, "Come".

Mason followed too like a hypnotized puppet. He was surprised to find the door ajar but there was no time for reason. He quickened his pace and started a half-run.

"Come" the boy called again as they crossed the street and entered the Fairborn mansion. They took a seemingly unending flight of stairs until they reached the top floor. The blood looked down from the stairs and said, "Come". This time, his voice was just as cold as he was.

"I won't be late. I won't be late, mom" he repeated, sobbing.

The boy rolled off the stairs; banging his head on each step as he fell and went limp. Mason stood on his toes too and tilted forward and made to fall down the stairs too but a strong arm gripped him.

"Mason!" It was the voice of his uncle. His uncle shook him roughly until he snapped out of the hypnotism. "What are you trying to do?"

His uncle took him home. Mason narrated the whole story to him and his uncle concluded it was best to discard the Fairborn items. Mason slept well in the next couple of days before he left to his house. He never stopped wondering though, and he never told his parents about it.

But they found out eventually. They found out on that day he screamed and punched the mirror.

STORY N.5: MYSTERY OF THE CORNFIELD

The birds chirped and Mary Fisher, sitting on the rickety chair out front, drank coffee and smiled. She almost started regretting the decision to sell the farmhouse. She liked it out here in the open; free from the noise of the city. She was a promising, young writer whose specialty in macabre stories had brought her acclaim.

She threw a handful of grain at the black pigeons that danced on the floor and they raced to it. Since she turned 18 and claimed ownership of the farmhouse - a property she inherited from her dead father - she had always spent the summer holidays here. It had served as a getaway countless times. But this would be her last. Her very last day, in fact. She had reached an agreement with the Anderson's to sell the property.

She took a long look at the house. A wave of sadness washed over her. Part of her felt like she was relinquishing the last memory of her father. In fact, the last few days had been filled with very strange dreams. In the first dream, she had seen herself tied to a dry beanstalk just inches away from the scarecrow that suddenly shook and came to life. The scarecrow had reached for head with a sickle. That day she woke up sweating like she had been thrown in a pool; her bed sheet was soaked in her sweat.

In her diary, she recorded the dream in red ink and made a mental note to use it in one of her stories. The next day, the dream was different. This time, she saw herself in the basement covered in dust. She wasn't shaken by this particular dream but it stuck to her mind more than any other. She just assumed it was her mind's way of saying 'don't leave'.

She strolled through the cornfields and let the blades of rice lightly caress her fingers. A cloud had gathered above and she was sure there was going to be a downpour. She ran indoors when the wind started to sing an angry song. From her front yard, she watched the wind sweep through the farm; bending the blades of rice and the weak scarecrow.

"Such power!" she said out loud.

The wind blew her dress too and slammed all the open windows shut. Even the cowbells in the empty cow pens jingled loudly; the jingling became solemn as the fierceness of the wind waned. Then it rained in torrents.

The wind messed with the power cables so the light went out. She lit a candle on her reading table and brought out one of her favorite novels and read. Her reading was constantly interrupted by the clattering of metal railings of the gates and the bright flashes that filtered through the space beneath the door.

The candlelight was so dull that it lulled to her sleep. Another dream started. This one had her in the field running away as fast as her legs could carry her and a figure chasing after her. The dry plants tore her cheeks and legs as she ran, they blocked her sight and wrapped around her legs almost as if there was a conspiracy to thwart her escape from the evil she was running from. The figure she couldn't see swooped down on her as she fell.

She woke up with a gasp. The chase had felt so real that she could still feel the saltiness in her mouth. It was a feeling she was familiar with. It was like the one she felt when she was writing horror stories; it was the taste of thrill.

The candle had been blown off by the heavy gust of wind blowing in. The pages of her novel too were flapping wildly and the empty can of beer she had drunk earlier fell to the ground. It took a moment for her to realize that the door had been blown open and two bright heads of light were pouring in.

She shook her lightheadedness off and went to the door. The light was from her car's headlights and this was a big surprise to her. She lifted her dress and ran in the rain into her car.

After turning off the lights and bolting the door, she managed to light another candle. She read for a while and headed to her room. One of the things she had always loved about the farmhouse was the quietness but this night, she felt it was deathly quiet and for no reason, she felt a sensation crawl under her skin.

The blanket of silence hanging over the house was soon torn apart by honks from her car. She sprang up from the bed and looked through the window and found that, in addition to the loud honking, the headlights were on again. Her body became cold now. If she hadn't been here, she would have assumed this was a scene cut off a story of hers.

She threw a scarf over her shoulder and went out again. Immediately she opened the door, the honking stopped and the headlight went off. She frowned a bit and held out the candle to check if anyone was lurking around. She would be very mad if she had found out someone was playing a prank on her. There was no one in sight and that wasn't unexpected since it was private property. The rain had stopped and so had the provoked wind yet she couldn't help but feel coldness approach.

As she turned to bolt the door a second time, her candle light went out and she was hit by a sharp gust of wind. The wind wrapped the scarf around her neck and a strange force dragged across the floor. Her screams were trapped in the tightness in her neck. She struggled frantically to untie the scarf but the grip was unnaturally tight. As she neared the threshold of her pain, the grip was released and she tried to run out of the house and zoom off into the darkness but the door snapped shut.

The saltiness returned to her mouth again and she crawled blindly into her room. She jammed the door and rested her back against it.

The house was so quiet that her rapid panting echoed. But that was when she heard the strangest thing - a baby's cry. It sounded distant but it filled the vacuum of the night. She wiped her face that had become really sweaty despite the cold. The cries stopped and a digging sound followed. The digger must have been used to the process. The tuft-tuft-tuft of the digger against the soil came at regular interval. Images ran amok in Mary's mind and her heart rate tripled astronomically when she placed her ear onto the wooden floor and heard the sound coming from below her.

The digging lasted for a while and stopped abruptly. Mary scrambled on to the stool by her bed to find another candlestick. Luckily, she did. And for the third time, she lighted one again.

Knock!

Knock!

Knock!

Her door rattled. She climbed into her bed and covered herself with a duvet.

Knock!

Knock!

Knock!

Mary lay on the bed like a felled log of wood and dug her fingers into the pillow.

Knock!

Knock!

She waited for the third knock but none came. Instead, the locked door creaked open slowly. By this time, Mary could hear her teeth clattering as she waited her death. The floor gave way and she dropped into the basement with her bed; screaming as she fell. The baby's cry had now become a soft but eerie laughter. She rolled to the ground, just like she had envisioned herself in her dream. She rolled; pulled by a force and fell into the hole that had been dug by the strange figure with a digger.

The first heap of dust landed on her face, then on her thigh until she was neck-covered in dust. The light; one whose origin she wasn't sure of, illuminated the face of the shadowy figure dully. It was her father in his farm clothes. She thrashed about under the light weight of dust like a beheaded snake.

"Father, look at me... Please. Stop this, please"

She kept on repeating and the cackle of the baby increased too.

When the soil was finally tossed at her face, she screamed and woke up.

Light from the sun scorned her forehead and she squinted her eyes. She lifted her face from the floor and when her eyes opened eventually, she shot up and looked around. What was she doing lying down in the field? She had been there all night.

She tried to remember all that had happened the night before but they were blurry and her head hurt. The dream was still clear though. The cry and laughter of the baby reverberated in her ear and she felt a shudder run through her. She ran to the house and on the reading table was an old bottle of liquor. She had no memory of her drinking from the dirty bottle but she assumed it must have been responsible for the vivid visions. She doubted this and truly, two years later, after the new people had moved in, their adolescent daughter started to have the same dreams and when she told her parents there was a baby in the basement calling at her, they waved it off.

Until it took her.

She never got the chance to ask her mom what Mary Fisher was doing in their basement, crying like a baby.

STORY N.6: OCTOBER 30TH

When Mr. Zuma's family moved to the United States, his son, Ali, found it harder to settle. The new culture coupled with the weather and the high schools had all been too much for him to process. He was the introvert in his class, the one who came and left as quietly as nothingness. But the Halloween had brought him out. He had planned to spend the whole evening in his room with his Xbox. That was until he saw the poster plastered onto his locker in school. It was an invitation to a Middle school Halloween party after school.

"Hey, Ali!" his friend, Mike, said, barging into him.

"Hey..." Ali replied but screeched when he saw Mike's mask. "You freaked me out"

The students in the hallways had all turned to him but he bowed his head and tried to hurry out of the building.

"Ali! Wait up!" Mike ran after him, pulling his mask off. "I am sorry, c'mon!"

"You made fun of me in front of everyone" Ali growled.

"I am sorry. I know I was a jerk but listen to me"

"What's it this time?"

"You know, it's going to be your first Halloween. Do you have a costume yet?"

Ali shook his head in the negative.

"Um, so what are you going to wear then? Have you even thought of that?"

"I was thinking of staying indoors" was his bland reply but Mike's disappointed look made him change his mind. "But I do not even have a costume"

"We can get you a mask! Like mine"

"I don't know...that would be...nice, I guess"

"So, it's settled then" Mike grinned.

**

"Now that's scary!" his father commented, when Ali came out of his room all dressed and painted.

His little sister shrieked.

"OK. I will be back after the party" Ali said, and ran off to meet Mike. He had caught the fever too.

The street was full of people in similar costumes; it was a sea of red, blue and black.

"This time of the year, Gotham goes gothic" Mike commented in his comic way, as they walked with the other kids creating fear and demanding candy.

Most of the adults simply laughed and feigned horror. A bigger boy rushed towards them in the most horrific costume Ali had seen and grabbed the candy they had just collected from their hands. The boy had a mask that was fitted with long, pointy horns and mouth that displayed fangs when he opened them.

"That was a costume too?" Ali said, panting after they had all ran a distance. Mike laughed and said, yes.

"Of course, it is. Brace yourself. You are going to see worse" Mike added, trying to catch his breath.

"There's a Halloween gathering down the road. Let's go!" another boy announced and they all went there, veering from their initial course to the school party.

Ali feared that, with all he had seen, he would never be able to sleep again. There were two dead deers on the floor that had bite injuries on their neck. The bigger boy they had seen earlier was there too; and with a couple of his friends all dressed similarly.

Rock music blared from the speakers and the place was so dense with smoke that he couldn't see clearly - it was like a haze. The building had been decorated for the season; pumpkins that appeared to bleed hung on the walls and there were makeshift compartments in the house. Each of them had a form of horror.

Some were boys with animal heads or animal hooves, others were filled with sick-looking people who sprawled on the floor like they were going to die any moment, then there were zombies making disgusting guttural sounds too. Ali and Mike pushed through the thick crowd and they made their way through to the makeshift counter where some lady with thick bat cloaks served a fizzy drink in a brown paper cup.

"Not alcoholic" she said, giving them a toothy grin, when she noticed their reluctance to drink.

Ali sniffed the drink and poured it down his throat. It tasted a lot like soda. When he turned round, he saw that Mike was going to check on something else. He made to follow him but he changed his mind and decided that he had walked enough for one night so he sat on a short, red bench and, with his face between his palms, watched the wild crowd.

The crowd started to reduce slowly and strangely because he had not seen anyone leave through the closed doors. Could it be the sleep threatening to shut his eyes or did he just see a boy biting another, he wondered. He searched the building for Mike but couldn't find him or any of the other boys he had come with. The fog in the place thickened and Ali gave up. There was no way he was going to find Mike in this cloud. He could still hear people screaming and shrieking so he figured the fun was still on somewhere.

And again, he saw a boy dragged on the floor and two others swooped on him. They crouched by his side and sunk their fangs into his neck. Ali rubbed his hands over his eyes and looked again but the fog had gathered. When it cleared, there was no sign of any absurdity. The music still blared and the singers still struck their guitar with the same mad fervor but Ali, at this point, couldn't help but notice the significant reduction in the house. It was clearer now. The crowd had thinned so much that people could move freely. Yet he could not remember ever seeing anybody leave. He stood up and made for the door.

"Party isn't over yet! Shouldn't you wait for your friend -" the batty girl who had served them the drink said.

"Friend?"

"Yes, Mike. Was that - I mean, *is* that his name?"

"Yea..." Ali said, collapsing back on the bench. "Seen him around?"

"Yes. Some moments ago... Right, Iva?"

Ali followed her eye to see who she had called Iva. It was a very big boy with a mask that was just as horrific as that of the guy that had snatched their candy – only bigger. Iva sat on a chair close to the door and drummed his long, dark fingers on the table.

"Yes, some moments ago" Iva said, with a deep baritone voice.

"See? Relax; they will be here for you soon"

But Ali couldn't relax. The candy bag that had been snatched from them was on the table where Iva sat. There were more screams and shouts from the compartments. From his bench, there were not more than ten people left and each time a person went into a compartment, they never seemed to come out. Something was off, he was sure.

"Another drink?" the girl offered. She still had her grin plastered – one that Ali now found creepy. Ali collected the cup from her with hands so shaky that he spilled half the drink. The drink was much warmer than he could remember and just when he gulped it, the music stopped.

The deafening silence in the place resonated louder than the music ever had. He looked up and there was no rock band on the platform anymore and the red- haired disk jockey wasn't there either.

"OK, I think the party is over now" Ali said, wiping imaginary dust away from his buttocks. He kept the paper cup on the counter and looked from girl at the counter to Iva. Iva had been still; watching him. There was a hunger in his eyes that Ali couldn't understand.

Iva beckoned on him with his long forefinger. Ali swallowed the lump that had formed in his throat and walked towards Iva.

"Chill! Sit down and let's devour this bag of candy" he said and cracked his knuckles.

There was no way that wasn't the bag of candy they had collected earlier, Ali thought. They sat opposite each other and ate the candy slowly. The girl cleaned up the counter and struck a conversation with three other boys who had come out of the compartment. They spoke in low tones but Ali could make out the words, "one left", "for Iva", "clean up this mess". He shuddered.

Meanwhile, Iva's gaze never left him.

"So how was the party?"

"What?" Ali asked – his attention elsewhere.

"The party... How was it?"

"Good, I guess"

"Better than you expected?"

"Yes" Ali lied. He was horrified. He mouthed more candy than his mouth could hold; he figured this would allow him leave the place as quick as possible.

"So it's your first ever Halloween..." Iva said.

Ali wasn't quite sure that was a question and he was distracted by the other boys and the counter girl who had now formed a circle behind him. He nodded three quick times and mouthed, yes.

The others giggled.

"I think I should get going" Ali said and stood up and headed for the door.

"No, not that way. Take the back door. That's where the others followed" Iva boomed.

"Oh...Thanks for the candy, too."

He quickened his steps. He suddenly realized how dark it had been. When he tried to open the door, he was met with a stiff resistance. The door wouldn't open. He was going to turn around and call them for help but when he did turn around, they were already there; Iva in front. He could have sworn he didn't hear their footsteps approach.

"The... The door..."

Iva didn't say anything. He just walked towards Ali. Ali moved back until his back was against the wall. Iva smiled and turned his head between his hands until it made a crack.

"Let's hope you taste better than the candy" he said and clasped his hand around Ali's throat. Ali felt his feet lift from the floor. Ali screamed and kicked wildly at him. When Iva's face drew closer and he showed his fangs, Ali held onto the horns on his head and tried to pull the mask off but he got the horror of his life! It was no mask! He was a real monster.

Nobody knows what happened on October 30th. Nobody knows. But they know the monsters are still at large.

STORY N. 7: LAST MAN ON EARTH

You are the last man on earth; not even your dog made the cut or your mom. But before this, you are driving home on the eve of your 18th birthday. It was rainy and the visibility was poor. You were driving a little too fast for no reason. You liked the thrill and that's why you couldn't step on the brakes on time. She had come out from nowhere. She wasn't looking and when you honked, she turned sharply. She was holding a doll amongst many other things. She looked and screeched just about the same moment that your mom's car screeched and blood covered the screen. You lost control.

But, now, you are in your house. The TV has gone dead; so has electricity. Outside, snowflakes falls steadily like cotton and from your house you can see the end of the street. The houses are quiet too, and no smoke is rising from any chimney. Your door is hanging loose. Something must have pulled it off its hinges but you don't know what. There's nothing that could be seen and perhaps, it's the wind that has wreaked the havoc. For your sake, you hope it is the wind. It is a safer evil. There could be nothing worse than having a wild animal on rampage as lone partner in an empty world. The kitchen is empty too. The fridge; like the TV; dead. Flies swarm out when you open the door and the stench of rotten meat fills your nostrils. You shut the door and your face squeezes into a frown. You hiss.

A toolbox lies open on the table in the sitting room. You pick nails and a hammer from it and set to fix the door. As the hammer strikes, the sound echoes and returns like the ripples of a wave heading for the shore. The sound is deathly; each hit sounds like a church clock striking 12. You stop as you have a fear that the sound might wake up the dead.

You head out – the snow makes squelch-squelch sounds as you step on them. It sounds as though there is someone walking behind you but when you turn, there is nothing; no one; just an extra pair of foot prints walking behind yours! You freeze.

"Come out of your hiding!" you holler. There's no answer. You watch the foot prints walk past you ...left, right; left, right. And you follow the trail.

The street looks even more desolate than before; especially with the wide sweep of snow. The neon light on the motel's billboard is dull and cars lined the streets; some of them parked at the centre of the road. The foot prints lead you to a house - a dark house. You hear a flutter of wings and from the window, an army of bats fly out and you duck.

"What in God's name happened here?" You ask yourself. You are curious but too scared to go into the house and check. You turn around and head for the convenience store instead. There is a sign out front saying "Closed" but the door is ajar. Packs of sweet and groceries litter the floor. A lot of goods have been destroyed and at the meat stand, you find that the meat has been ravenously eaten but you know not by what. Even coins are everywhere now from the cash register; but who needs money. You still stuff a handful of pennies into your coat pocket. There's nothing else in the cash register.

Then, you hear a sound. It is coming from a room that has a plaque above the door saying "Staff only". The voices are indistinct and even though you had your ear to the door, you couldn't make out what was being said. You turn the knob and push the door open - and out ran rats! A million of them storm out after you. They are the biggest rats your eyes have ever seen. They are as big as cats. You are the last piece of meat on earth so you run without looking back. If you had looked back, you would have seen the other two people staring angrily at you but you don't see them.

You run into a car and one of the rats jump in after you – it sinks its teeth into your laps but you fling it out. There is no blood coming out from you and you are shell-shocked. The teeth marks are there though. You try to hot-wire the car but the battery is dead. Outside, the rats are eating the rubber off the tyres. You open the door and run away. Other cars are dead too. Expect one. You hear it revving – the engine is on.

There is blood on its windshield and it is cracked badly. You recognize the car because it is your mom's but you don't remember driving up here. You wonder where the blood came from. You drive through the streets after you start the screen wiper. With each swipe, you see a woman – a flash of her. You try to turn the music player on but there is no music playing. The radio stations are dead – only static sounds but as you turn the knob slower, you pick up a signal. A man and a woman are talking.

"It is him. He did it. He saw me on the road and he did it!" the woman says, her voice hollow. "He has to go too. He just has to. You understand?"

"Are you sure?" the male voice says. His voice is hoarse.

Static interrupts again – everything is quiet for a while. You turn the radio knob furiously and try to reestablish connection. The voices swim in and out and you can't hear a thing. And then it becomes clear again. Parts of the conversations were lost.

"… of course, he lives down the street!" the woman says, anger now evident in her voice. Down the street? You wonder.

"Alone?" the man asks.

"Yes"

"How do you know?"

"I was with him earlier – before he left. I took him to my house. He didn't have the decency to enter"

"Before he left?"

"Yes, to the convenience store - before the rats chased him"

Your eyes pop out of its socket. You are threading the pieces and linking them to form a whole. Are they talking about you? You tighten your grip on the steering wheel.

"It was him? Then we must deal him the blow"

"Yes. He listens to us as we speak this moment" the woman says. There's a hysterical laughter.

You turn the radio off and step on the brakes. For a moment you wait, but you when you try to restart the car, it doesn't start! It is stuck in the thick snow. You walk aimlessly around and when the cold starts to become severe, you decide it is time to go home. Your mind wanders to what you've heard over the radio. There was no one else they could have been talking about but you - and why? You walk past the house where you had earlier seen bats fly from. It was just as dark as it had been earlier but now you can see the blood on the porch. You walk past it and past the store and the rats are still eating the tyres of the parked vehicles; some had moved to devouring the chassis. The skies are darkening and evening is fast becoming night.

"What!" You exclaim as you reach home to find multiple foot prints on your snowy lawn.

Your door is still hanging loosely open. You are scared to go in but the cold is not your friend so you shakily walk in.

It's almost as quiet as you had left it but the fireplace is crackling with fire.

"Hello!" you call. There is no response!

You walk towards the fireplace and sit. The warmth fights the cold that had seeped into your bones. You are relaxed - until you feel the grip of a bony hand on your shoulder. You scream and turn back. Then, you see the two of them - man and woman. They are a stark contrast. While the man is dressed in a thick black cloak, the woman is dressed in a bloodied hospital gown.

She is holding a black doll. The same black doll - you can't remember where but you feel in your subconscious that you had seen the doll somewhere. Fear grips you. They don't say anything - they just look at you. The man had dark eyes and he smelled like burnt wood. He smelled like the fireplace.

"You are ready?" he says, - or asks, you are not sure.

"Ready!" you stutter. His mouth is like coal.

As you say this, they fade away and you see a blinding light from a bulb above. You are in a hospital bed and there are doctors in lemon-green gowns with surgical masks looking over you - the view is blurry. There is blood and they are stitching you up. You black out. Voices become distant in your head. They float in and out - the woman's, the man's and the voices of the doctors.

When you wake, you are still in the hospital. You are dizzy. Had it all been a dream? People troop in to wish you quick recovery. They say your car tumbled and the woman died eventually. The doctors couldn't save her. You weep and ask for a picture of the woman. Your mom shows you. The eyes are looking directly at you - it's haunting. It's the bloodied woman in your head. It all clicks. The woman you hit! You feel you are being watched. There are eyes everywhere - you can feel it.

In the basket where people came to drop flowers and get-well-soon cards, you see the black doll amongst them. You cringe.

"Excuse me! Who placed this here?" you ask the nurse.

"A man... He's outside. Should I call him in?" she asks.

"Yes, please"

She leaves and speaks to someone outside. The man stops at the door and stares in through the glass on the door. You see him - he's the man in your head, the woman's accomplice. He is wearing a black coat now. He nods and leaves. Somehow, you know this is not over. Because as you leave for home a month later, you dog doesn't run to your side as usual. It cowers and scurries away after it sniffs your clothes.

"Hey, it's just me" you say to it, as it hides behind the couch. An ominous aura thickens in the house. You take off your coat and you hear something jingle in your pockets. You dip your hands into the pocket and bring out a handful of pennies - it was the ones you had stuffed into your pocket at the convenience store. You shudder - what is it still doing in your pocket?

You lay on your bed and under your blanket, you feel a movement. You sit up sharply and scream. It was one of the big rats from the store that was on your bed. It squealed - you blink and it is not there anymore. When you look up, you see them again - the man and the woman in the same way they had appeared in your head. She glares and points at you. The man pulls out a scythe and you scream again. He touches your chest with the pointy end and they vanish.

In about the same time, your mom rushes into the room.

"Sonny, what's wrong? Sonny, wake up" she cries.

"I am fine, mom. It's over. They are gone" you say.

But, your mom is still crying. She gives your body another shake.

"Wake up, sonny. Don't do this" she cries.

"I am awake!" you are confused. You try to touch your mom's face but your hand passes through her like a beam of light. You scream in shock and stand up from the bed. You see your mom shaking the body on the bed. Then it hits you. You are dead.

STORY N.8: THE GIRL IN THE WOODS

I was just 9 years old when I first went to the woods with my father and uncle for camping. I was very excited about the trip - so excited that the night before it, I couldn't sleep. I got my boots out and polished it. My mother said it was of no use though.

"You don't polish boots when you are going to the woods. It's not a ball" she said, smiling at me.

When the day came, we set out early - way before the break of dawn. The grasses were wet and dew dropped on our faces. I had a small backpack and a camera. As we traveled, I made sure to take pictures of everything. From the chestnut trees to the yellow and brown mass of dead leaves. My father smiled. He could see how happy I was. Somehow, I was sure they (my uncle and father) were just as excited as I was on their first trip as boys too.

Every now and then, we stopped to take rests. We would sit by the foot of a tree and drink from our cans. There was a way the water tasted that made me feel like I had never drunk water in all my life. It tasted like fulfillment.

"Enjoying the trip?" my father asked, smiling.

He knew I was but he wanted to hear me say it.

"Of course, I do" I gushed.

They smiled and my uncle gave my head a rub. They started to talk about bearing, geography and where to camp for the night.

"There should be a clearing just ahead. We could set up a tent there" My uncle said, looking at a map.

We marched on and soon we were at the clearing like my uncle had said there would be. We built our tents and laid a mat on it and made a fire outside. In silence, we ate the salted meat we roasted over the camp fire. Our surrounding smelled meaty. As I ate, my eyes surveyed the entire clearing. I would have taken a picture because it actually is a beautiful place. The trees formed a circle around it. It made me feel like the place was revered or reserved for a greater purpose. As I looked further into the forest, my eyes caught a ghostly sight. I saw a little girl. I was going to call the attention of my father to it but it left before I could do so.

"I think I saw a girl just now" I said.

They looked at each other and laughed out loud like teenage boys.

"There is no-one here. Did your mother feed you camp stories?" my father replied, and laughed again.

"No, I honestly think I did see something"

"That always happens - especially on your first time camping. You see things" my uncle joined in.

"Remember how we thought we saw a girl on our first time out, too?" my father added.

Just then, a twig snapped. And we were all quiet for a while. My father narrowed his eyes and looked closely into the darkness. Then, he burst into laughter.

"Probably just a rabbit. Time to sleep. Don't let it get to you"

We brought some of the wood to the entrance of our tent and slept.

The night was quiet but for the occasional spark of fire and chirps of insects. I couldn't sleep. I had only seen the girl for a quick period but the image registered in my head. As I started to slip into sleep, I heard a twig snap outside and my blood curdled. There was a steady rustling of leaves. And footsteps neared the tent. I closed my eyes shut after I turned around and found my uncle and father fast asleep. I knew it had to be the girl I had seen earlier. I saw her shadow outside the tent. She blew out the fire and the whole place became dark. The light from the crescent only dimly illuminated the room. I was so scared I couldn't even move a muscle. Then, she sat down and crunched on the bones we had discarded on the floor. She ate slowly.

Then I heard her stand and walk a distance. It appeared she was standing in front of the tent because she blocked out the moonlight completely. I feared she could hear my heart drumming fast. She walked and stopped outside my side of the tent.

She was so close to it that I could hear breathing. Then, she spoke. Her voice almost sounded like a hiss.

"I don't have shoes. I have been walking this way for years"

I didn't say anything.

"I know you are awake" She said.

My palms became extremely sweaty. I still didn't say anything.

"Give me your shoes - the polished ones. I like them"

I trembled now. My father and uncle, even with all the noise, slept soundly. I took off my shoes, crawled to the mouth of the tent and dropped them there.

I later slept off. I partly believed all of that had transpired, happened in my dream. But when I woke up, my shoes were gone. My father said nothing about it. He was just puzzled. My uncle had suspicions though. I knew he could see it in my eyes that more had happened.

When I went home, I told my mom about the missing shoes but not about the girl in the woods. She took me to a store to get a new one. I found one that looked exactly like mine. They were so alike. I tried them on and like the former one, they were a perfect match but there was a paper on the bottom of the sole.

I read it in my room. It read:

"Thanks for the shoes. Can I keep your teddy bear?"

I rushed to my wardrobe to check for my teddy bear. There was none there.

STORY N.9: BECOMING

At the toy shop, the wolf silently stood in the section filled with toy animals. Its black fur glistened under the blue florescent light and its eyes glowed red like burning hot coal. Its thirst for blood had reached an incredible level - it was insatiable now. Children in the toy shop ran around pointing at the new toys in the shop.

"I thought you said you wanted a soldier figurine" one woman asked her son.

"Yes I want that but Mom, there are so many toys out here. I am not so sure what I want anymore. You are going to have let me take one more" the boy begged.

"It's not even your birthday yet" his mom teased him.

"Mom, look at the animal section. There are so many cool toys"

"I see..."

"Whoa! Mom, come see this! It's a large size wolf"

"That looks so real, wow! It's cool but there's no way I am getting that. It is too scary"

The boy moved close to the wolf and stroked its head and fur. The boy's scent filled the wolf's nose and a volcano erupted in its belly.

"If I had this - all of my friends would be so scared of me. It has actual fur. Mom, ask the attendant how much it costs"

When the attendant came, he shrieked and yelled for them to run!

"Run!"

***

Wilson could feel the *'thing'* crawling under his skin. It went from his belly, as usual, and moved up to his throat. He tried to swallow saliva so he could push it down but the burning sensation continued in his throat. He felt his chest tighten as though it would rupture in any minute.

The teacher's rap on his desk brought him out of his reverie.

"Everything all right, Mr. Wilson?" the teacher queried.

Wilson squeezed his eyes shut and said, "Yes, I am". The teacher and the rest of the class looked at him suspiciously.

"I called your name three times" the teacher said. "You look under the weather. You should go home and get some rest"

"I am..." Wilson was going to say he was fine but a sharp pain tore through his chest. "I am going home". He swung his school bag across his shoulder and left wincing. He stopped by at the school clinic and the nurse, after taking his temperature, looked at him strangely.

"Your temperature is...very low. Do you feel feverish?"

"I am burning on the inside"

"But the thermometer here is reading different. I mean, this is an abnormal temperature... if I hadn't seen that you were human, I would have probably thought you were a reptile or something else. You know what? Give me a moment"

As soon as the nurse left the room, he left the clinic and went home.

***

The whole incident had started three days ago at the hospital. He knew this was related to the bizarre event that happened at the hospital that day. He had had a chest burn; one that his mom feared could be a sign of ulcer. After tests, his doctor had written him some prescriptions to take to the nurse. At the nurse counter was a man he hadn't seen before at the hospital.

"Good morning! I was asked to bring this here"

The man had a stony face and mean demeanor and was more hairy than the average middle-aged man. He stared at the prescriptions and his face suddenly broke into a smile and he passed it onto another man who had been sitting quietly with him.

"Chest pain?"

"Yes"

"How old are you?

"18? Why?"

The men exchanged looks and grinned.

"Sounds perfect! You are going to have to come in" the hairy one said.

"Yes, for a shot!" the other one chipped in.

"They drew the curtains close when he came in and asked him to sit on the stretcher.

"Roll your sleeves up. This is going to sting, boy. But you'll be fine"

That injection changed everything. He felt a surge of power and fire but the chest pain subsided almost instantly.

"You are new here?" Wilson asked the nurse, who directed him to a pharmacy.

He was reluctant to answer but he finally said, yes. Wilson nodded and left.

When Wilson got home however, he discovered that he was not. At night, he felt really cold and shivered under his blanket. But that was only the beginning. He received an email that read:

"Venom active. Subject 001 experiences fever. Day 3/30"

The cryptic email came as a shock to him but not half as shocking as the picture of himself under the blanket that he received. And he was alone in the room! The sender was unknown.

He quickly looked round the room; checked his wardrobe for hidden cameras. There was nothing! When he looked out of his window, he saw a man but only for a second. The man had moved too fast for him to process the image. Almost superhumanly fast - one would think his body was a blur.

The days passed and every day, he got a picture with an email that stated the progress of the venom in his stream.

That day after he had returned from school, he came to terms the fact that he could be a lab rat in some creepy science experiment but to what end, he wondered.

"Venom takes form. Day 6/30".

The email came an hour before the venom actually took form in a bewildered Wilson. He writhed in pain and watched his veins bulge as an eel-like thing move through them. He threw his head backwards and groaned like an injured maniac.

"Everything okay in there, Willie?" his mom called, lightly knocking on his door. That was a question he would later get used to being asked.

Urgh, he groaned one last time and the pain subsided.

"Willie?" she called again, turning the knob this time but he had locked the door.

"Yes, mom. I am fine. Working out!" he replied.

"Isn't it too late for that?"

"Well..."

"Sleep well"

"I will. You too"

For reasons, he couldn't let his mom know about the strange happenings yet. She would freak out, he was sure. And somehow, he was protecting the venom. He didn't know why but he was. It was like he was being controlled. He felt the need to figure out everything before making his case known. On the fifteenth day, the thing moved to his chest and stretched to limits he didn't know existed. His mother and little sister exchanged looks when they heard him banging on his door upstairs.

"Looks like he's taking the whole workout thing hard on himself" his mother said. "Is he planning on becoming a boxer?"

"No way! He's planning on becoming truant. Do you know he stays away from school, mom?"

"What? Since when?"

"Two weeks ago, I was told"

"I need to sit that boy down..."

"By the way, why has he stopped joining us for dinner?" his sister asked.

"I...will talk to him" she resolved and they sat in silence.

Wilson slept off with the screen of his laptop showing a new email.

"Takeover complete. Phase II initiation".

His head felt too heavy for his neck. He had a dream where he was panting and running in a never-ending tunnel. He didn't see himself though; he could only gear his heavy footsteps. It was almost as though he was in a video game. He woke up with a maddening level of hunger and he went to the fridge.

"Looks like the "workout" is doing you a lot of good" his mom said as he closed the fridge and he almost dropped the jar of jam in flight.

"Mom!" he screamed. "You frightened me!"

"I didn't mean to"

"Why are you up?"

"To check up on you. What have you been up to lately?"

"Err... nothing" he replied casually.

"And what exactly keeps you away from school?"

He was going to reply when he caught a shadow moving outside the kitchen. The shadow stopped and the food stuck in Wilson's throat.

"Willie..." his mom waved her hand over his face and turned around to check what he was looking at. The shadow vanished.

"... I have just been unwell"

"Unwell? Should we go to a clinic tomorrow?"

"I don't think - well, ok"

When he went to his room, he rushed to the bathroom and dumped his head in the toilet; vomiting all he had just ate. He wiped his mouth and looked at the mirror. He realized his mom was right. He was looking sturdy and chiseled. He wiped his face with a towel and for a brief moment, his eyes were deep red.

Upon arriving at the hospital and booking an appointment, they sat at the guest waiting room. Wilson looked down the hall and standing was the same man who had administered the injection into him. He recognized him as the man that stood outside the house, this time, he didn't run or vanish. It was almost as though he was calling on him.

"Mom, give me a moment" he pleaded, heading down the hall towards the man.

"Be quick. It's almost our turn!" his mom replied.

As he neared the end of the hall, the man entered a ward and was gone. He stopped by the nurse station and the regular nurse, Ms. Brittany, was present.

"Hey, what about the other new guy?" Wilson asked her, after exchanging pleasantries.

"New guy?"

"New guys, I mean. There were two of them. They said they were new"

"You met them here?" Wilson knew now that they weren't medical personnel.

"Um, never mind" he said and left.

Wilson started to find the antiseptic smell disgusting. He could smell everything strangely; from the breath of the sick people, to the urine in the toilet, to the nurse's soft deodorant.

He walked out of the hospital and went home. All through his journey home, his head banged and he had to walk slowly on the sidewalk to avoid bumping into anybody.

He sat on his bed and covered his ears. He could hear virtually everything within the radius of the neighborhood; from the police radio, the music in the house next door and the clanking of metal in someone's sink.

He had his first argument with his mom that night. She was mad at him for leaving.

"I am fine now!" he said, feeling himself heat up.

"So you are a doctor now?" his mom fired back.

"I said I am fine now!" he yelled, and hit the dining table hard. He pushed his chair back and left to his room. His mom and sister were both taken aback by the outburst and even more surprised that the table collapsed.

"Transforming 27/30"

His email read.

He had not eaten in days. He felt his body stiffen and his back cracked. He fell on the floor; crouching like a tiger aiming to pounce on a prey. He grunted as his bones cracked in the most unusual places until he was completely hunched. His finger nails started to bleed and he started to convulse.

"Will... What's going on in there?" His mom asked.

"Go...away!!!" He grunted.

On thirtieth day, the mail he was sent fear into him. He could taste blood in his mouth. He thirsted for it. The picture had the words.

"Evaluation: successful. Subject: wild"

There was no picture of him that day - only a picture of blackness. The next day, they woke up to news of a policeman killed in the woods. On his bed sheet were streaks of blood. For the first time in weeks, he wasn't hungry. His sleep was, however, dominated by him running around in dark tunnels.

One day, he waited for his dreams to play out to the end. There were trails of bodies on the wet grasses in the woods. There was the police man's, the girl cycling in the wood and a host of others whose faces had appeared on TV recently – and his sister's.

No! He said, twisting and turning in his sleep.

A howl emerged from within him. He could hear his sister knocking on the door. As his skin became fur, he knew, then, what he was.

He knew he couldn't stay home. So he jumped out of the window and into the night. It was the night he raced to the toyshop.

SCARY STORIES: VOL. 2

STORY N. 1: Amnesiac

It's cold, so cold... Everything's blurry, everything's fading away. A car, a collision, a smile... Pain, blood, screaming... Everything's... fading... away...

Those were the only images flashing in his head, right before his eyes, every couple of seconds. Every time he tried to open his eyes he'd feel the pain and he'd fall back into the images. In a way, they seemed to help him; they'd take away the pain, even though only momentarily, they'd take away everything, pulling him out of the painful reality and making him repeatedly see those images over and over again.

After what felt like a century, something happened, a new image popped in front of his eyes. It was... blue eyes. The bluest he had ever seen. This time, the pain was gone, the discomfort was gone too and he felt... whole again.

He opened his eyes all the way now, noticing the look on the woman's face. She was definitely pleased with herself; her smile was so kind and innocent, almost like a child's. But this peace was about to be disrupted by the noises that followed shortly after. It was screeches of joy, coming from the slightly opened door.

Two children that didn't seem to be older than 10 years old each rushed into the room, immediately jumping on the bed, hugging him. Their faces, he didn't know, in fact, he didn't know anything anymore. Before he could question anything the woman with blue eyes started talking while holding up a notepad.

"Welcome back to the land of the living, mister Richard. Glad to have you back with us." She said, with the same kindhearted smile on her face.

"R... Richard?"

"Yes, that is your name, isn't it? Immediately after you were hospitalized your wife immediately called and started asking about you. You were hurt pretty badly too, several contusions alongside a few broken ribs and internal bleeding. Honestly I'm surprised you woke up so easily, most patients would be comatose for at least a few weeks after suffering so many injuries."

"I... see."

"Don't strain yourself, you're still recovering. For the following couple of days you should avoid speaking too much and you should stay in bed as much as possible. Your memories will also be gradually coming back, no severe brain injuries were recorded so after a month or so you should be back to being yourself again. For now though, relax."

He nodded. "Richard..." he whispered to himself over and over again. It sounded familiar, but still there was something off about it. Before he could ask the doctor anything else another figure seemed to appear in the room. A woman, about as tall as him, brown hair and brown eyes. She was stunning, to say the least, but that's not what made him freeze for a second. There was a general sense of unease from the moment she walked in simply because he didn't actually see her walk in. She seemed to just... morph into the room.

Again, before he could say anything the woman started walking towards him, slowly, gradually getting closer and closer to his face until she seemed to be one centimeter away from touching his face with her nose. She looked at him, analyzing his facial expressions before a tear started running down her left cheek.

"You... idiot... you damned idiot. I told you to stay home, I told you to stay home." She whispered as more tears started rushing down her face before turning away from him and starting to hug the nurse. "Thank you Karen, thank you for saving my idiot of a husband again."

"It's become quite a tradition around, hasn't it? This time's rough though Jane, he could have lost his life. Honestly I'm surprised he's still in one piece after all's said and done."

"It's because of this new job he's got, you know how it is."

"Yeah, yeah, I get it. Just make sure he gets back to being himself and don't go too rough on him. He's already had a near death experience already; he doesn't need to experience more."

"If only it were that easy..." she whispered as both women started laughing.

All of that happened several days ago. The more he thought about it all though the more it seemed to not add up. Something was wrong, something felt out of place. The name Richard didn't sound recognizable at all, his name wasn't Richard, his name was...

The door opened yet again, and as per usual the woman seemed to be just standing in the middle of the room, staring at him. Her facial expression was the same, blank. Despite her laughing before, she didn't actually seem to smile, ever. She would look at him, analyze his every move, and point at a bunch of pills on the counter. She wouldn't leave unless he swallowed them, which he did every time. One time he wouldn't do it, but the more time passed the more pain he felt. After he did swallow them though, she'd disappear the same way she showed up.

None of it made sense, he knew that much. Maybe he was still recovering from the accident and he was making it all up as he went along, but there was still something about this that made him feel unsafe. Eventually, he picked himself up, started walking around the empty room. He knew he had no chance of outrunning anything outside of the room as he was, so he decided to focus on exercising before making a run for it.

He knew that the creature pretending to be a woman wasn't going to hurt him, she was just inspecting him, seeing if he was doing anything out of the ordinary. Eventually, after what seemed to feel like a century, he finally recovered most of his strength. He looked at the counter which had a bunch of pills on it as per usual. He picked them up and put them in his pockets, just in case the pain would come back.

He opened the door and looked outside, carefully trying not to attract any unwanted attention. No one was around, not a single being in sight. He sighed precariously and started walking around with his back against the wall to make sure nobody could sneak up on him. He walked and he walked until he eventually saw another door. He looked through the window when he saw a familiar face. The lady with the blue eyes.

She was saying something to another man that was lying on the bed. All of a sudden, he felt ill. The pain was slightly coming back and it was really starting to affect him. His legs felt weak for a second and as he tried to pull out the pills from his pocket he dropped them down.

He leaned towards the door, gasping for air, until he saw it. The scene that he had seen before had changed drastically. The woman with the blue eyes had changed. Everything was different. The woman's hair changed from a normal shade of blonde to what seemed to be black hair that hadn't been washed in years. It was all clamping to her cheeks. Her doctor outfit was also different. It was rugged, ripped apart in some places even. The patient was the same, but the machines that were seemingly keeping track of his health were now dead. Instead of talking all that he could hear was noises that he had never heard before. It was a mixture of cackling and teeth grinding.

The scene overall had made him sick, so much so that he immediately fell to his knees. Noticing that this could attract the attention of the doctor he immediately locked the door just in case she'd attempt to get out. The pain started dulling and after a couple more minutes he picked himself back up, only to fall back down when he spotted that the creature posing as a doctor was staring directly at him through the window.

Slowly, the door handle started turning. It turned and it turned until it all stopped. Shocked by what had happened right in front of him he felt paralyzed for a couple of seconds. The only reason as to why he was able to move afterwards was the fact that he heard another door open in the distance.

He immediately came back to his senses and started crawling away. The adrenaline in his body allowed him to run for what seemed like miles at the time. He ran until he eventually fell down on his knees, gasping for air. Tears had started running down his cheeks now as he started facing his situation. He was alone, he had no idea who he was and worst of all, he did not know what was real and what wasn't anymore.

He started breathing in and out, in and out, until he eventually couldn't help but fall on his back grasping his chest for air. He stayed there for a good couple of minutes until he heard footsteps around him. He closed his eyes for a second and the moment that he opened them back up the woman was back.

This time around though, she no longer had brown eyes and brown hair, quite the contrary actually. She had black eyes, as black as night itself, her hair was pale white, it resembled spider nets more than hair, and her mouth was always stuck in the same position. She was smiling from ear to ear, she was smiling. That smile immediately made him remember his accident, how it happened and who the culprit was.

She was there; she was the one that caused it all to happen. She ran into him and she made all of this happen. His breathing had become even more irregular, he was grasping onto his chest harder than before and before he knew it he passed out.

He woke up back in the bed, but this time around his hands and feet were strapped to the bed. After struggling for a good couple of minutes to escape he gave up, lying back on the bed waiting for the inevitable to happen. The door started creaking once again. He didn't even bother looking at it until he felt a sudden pain hit.

What he saw made him screech out loud. The two creatures that seemed to resemble children were not children after all. They were two extremely pale creatures wearing nothing, with holes for mouths. They had no eyes, no noses, no ears, just the pitch black mouths. Inside those mouths was what seemed to be just a long spiky tongue which would drag across the mattress as they came closer and closer to his face.

He closed his eyes and relaxed his body. There was no escape, no happy ending, he was going to die no matter what. Then, right as he felt one of the creature's saliva run across his cheeks he heard a faint voice call out to him.

"Father... are you okay?"

Tears started falling down his cheeks yet again. When he looked down the creatures were all staring right at him, grabbing his clothes and pulling on them so hard that they made it hard for him to even breathe anymore. He felt like he was losing consciousness yet again but he was instantly pulled out of it when he heard one of the creatures whimper.

The creatures were... crying. It was so surreal that it took him a second to process everything that was happening. These things, whatever they were, actually believed him to be their father. From that moment on he knew exactly what he had to do. He put on the kindest smile he could, all things considered, and before he knew it he was looking directly at the two creatures.

"Of course I am, since you're here. How's your day been so far?"

The two's eyes started glaring yet again, even though you couldn't decipher what they were actually thinking at the moment it was obvious that they were no longer in anguish.

"It's been fun. Mommy took us outside today; we heard you were sent to bed because you were bad so we figured we'd cheer you up. Are you hungry, daddy?"

"Oh, I'm starving, really. I've been munching on these pills all day long. Could you bring daddy a sandwich or something? That would make daddy way happier" he said, with a slight hesitation when it came to referring to himself as the father of the two.

The creatures stopped for a second. They got up and before he knew it they were gone. Regardless of whether he did something good or not, he couldn't help but feel happy that he was alone yet again. Whatever they were, they were still just babies, meaning he could still use them to get out. It was simple, get your strength back, make them release you and voila, freedom has been regained.

He sighed in relief, until he heard a loud thump on the ground. He tried to maintain his composure but what he saw next almost made him vomit the little he had eaten before. The two were back, but they weren't alone this time. A broken, mangled body was now spread across the floor. The arms and legs seemed to be all tangled about as if he had been dragged around for kilometers behind a car. On his face lied a huge bite mark, exposing his pink slimy brain.

Before he could say anything though, the body started moving, convulsing about as if being controlled by a sadistic puppeteer on a string. After seeing this, the two started cackling as if they'd just seen a standup comedian make a really funny joke on screen or something.

"W….w…. What have you done?!"

The two looked at him for a good couple of seconds confused at his lack of enjoyment over the scene that was unfolding before him.

"You said you were hungry, so we brought you food."

"W… who is he and where did you get him from?!" shouted the man.

"He's our former daddy. He was bad, he tried to run away so mommy made sure he could never run again."

"I… see…" said the man, as his life seemed to leave his body. "So, we eat humans, is that it?"

The two stared at him yet again, shocked at the words that were coming out of his mouth.

"You said you were hungry, right? So, eat." Said the smaller one as he ripped off the poor man's arm and threw it on the bed.

The man didn't even flinch anymore. He just stopped moving altogether. His eyes were dead set on the ground in front of him. He… snapped. His eyes were looking dead ahead of him and yet he didn't seem to be able to see anymore. He just, stopped thinking, he stopped moving, and it was quite shocking that he even continued breathing anymore at that point.

He stood there, for a good couple of hours, just staring at the arm. At one point the creatures left and the mother figure came back in. It stared at him until eventually she left too. Days seem to pass, and yet the man still wouldn't move. He no longer felt hungry, sad or terrified. He no longer felt anything, until it happened.

One day, after what seemed to feel like years had passed, he started smirking. That smirk turned into a smile and that smile started covering his whole face. He started laughing, laughing without stopping until the room was filled with all of the creatures that had tormented him so far. They were all inspecting him, trying to decipher what had caused this malfunction.

The laughter turned into cackling, it turned into what sounded like a screeching, convulsing with every high pitch sound that came out of his mouth. His laughter seemed to surprise the creatures, as they all came closer and closer to him. They all crawled onto the bed, getting closer and closer to the shell of a broken man that he was, creeping up on him, similar to how a lion is getting closer and closer to its prey.

The mother untied his hands as the two other creatures untied his legs. The man immediately grabbed his face and fell on his back. After releasing him the crowd started laughing too, each having a distinct laughter of themselves. The mother figure resembled the cackling of an old lady, the younger child like one had a very high pitch squeak-like laughter while the other young one sounded like simple breathing in and out of its nose, as if it didn't have the air to actually make a sound anymore.

After a couple of minutes of what seemed to resemble an orchestra of screeches and growls, the man stopped and just as sudden as they all started they all stopped too. The dead silence continued, until the man opened his lips.

"I... am home, my lovelies."

STORY N. 2: Midnight Train Ride

Nothing but deafening silence surrounded the pitch darkness around him, so much so that he felt like he was choking in it. He sat there, on the metal ground, convulsing every now and then. This lasted for what seemed to be an eternity, until a bright light blinded him. But for that short second that that light passed him by he managed to get a glimpse of his surroundings. There were two benches and 2 huge windows. Next to the windows was a huge dark curtain that was long enough to touch the ground. The windows were completely dark outside of the beacon of hope that had just passed by. After the darkness settled back in, he regained his senses and managed to get up on one of the benches. He was all out of breath after that feat. He felt like his own body wasn't cooperating with him anymore.

"W... Who... Where am... I?" He whispered to himself.

The deafening quietness was broken apart by a rhythmic sound outside of his little cage. Footsteps. His mouth opened wide and before he knew it he threw himself back down on the ground. He started crawling towards the metal door, inch by inch, getting closer and closer to it. But before he could actually scream for help or even knock on the door, a sudden gust of fear hit him. The footsteps didn't sound right anymore. They weren't footsteps. They sounded more like hydraulic presses crushing the ground with each thump. They sounded too rhythmic, too solid and too far away to be so loud. But that was about to change, because the sounds were getting closer and closer, louder and louder. At one point even the ground started shaking, signifying that whatever was out there was getting closer. Noticing this, he started backing away from the door. He was crawling back, step by step, trying not to alert them of his presence, until the thumps suddenly stopped. The quietness lasted for a good couple of minutes, until a loud metallic scrape sound made him cover his ears. It was the sound of a very heavy door being opened, no, being forced open. A series of cries for help followed the sound. By listening to the person's voice for a couple of seconds he could guess that the victim was a man, young, perhaps in his early 20s, being dragged out of his own little cell. The crushing sounds came back afterwards, but they were obviously going away this time, until the silence returned.

After he took a few heavy breaths, he got back up. He knew what he had to do now. If he was to escape this place, he needed to wait for those things to get back and force his way through. No... forcing wasn't the correct word for it. What he needed was to crawl himself out. He was good at that. Every time his dad busted into his room at night, looking for a way to blow some steam off he knew how to get out unscathed. This was the first time in his life that he was grateful for something that his dad taught him.

So, without wasting any precious time, he decided to devise a plan. He looked at his surroundings, anything that he could use, really. Two heavy looking metal benches and a pair of long curtains were the only things around. Nothing else. He then proceeded to look into his pockets, his clothes, literally anything else that could help him. He found a couple of nickels in his pocket alongside a wallet. After opening it he saw a strange person in there. That... wasn't him. But if it wasn't, then who was he? Who... was he? This sudden realization made him lose his footing once again. He was speechless.

"I'm... who... Of course I'm... I have a w... daugh-". He kept whispering, while biting his own lips after every word. But before he could answer his own questions, the loud thumps were back.

He was literally broken out of his confusion. Nothing else mattered, except getting out of there. So he got back up and he started pulling on the benches. The sound that came from them being moved almost cut his sanity in half. The loud screeching of the floor made him pull even harder, until he managed to put them right next to the windows. He then proceeded to pull the other bench there, but this time he used all of his strength to lift it and put it on top of the other bench. He then took the curtain and put it over the benches. He was sweating more than ever before in his life, he knew that much. That bench must have weighed at least 100kg. As a little cherry on top, he decided to put his shoes right under the benches, so that it looked like his feet were sticking out from underneath. Together, the two benches should keep the guards occupied enough to allow him to run out through the door.

With his plan successfully laid out, he decided to wait behind the door, stuck to the wall. The thumps were getting closer and closer, until he couldn't hear anything anymore. Suddenly, the door started moving. The screeching sound it made almost made him fall back on the ground, but luckily enough the door pushed him back towards the wall. The loud steps entered the room. The figures were so tall they had to bend over to actually enter the room. There were two of them. When they spotted the little contraption that he made, a deafening cackle began. This absolutely terrified him. The cackling filled the entire cell, until the creatures stopped and started moving closer and closer to the benches. He could have run out right then and there, but when he tried to, his body didn't listen to him anymore. The creatures didn't even seem human anymore based off of the noises they were making. The sudden movements they made were followed by cracking noises, as if they were literally breaking their bones to move around. They had spotted the shoes on the ground. One of the creatures leaned over and started getting closer and closer to them. Then, all of a sudden, the light came back through the windows. The curtains covered most of it up, but it was just enough to actually get a glimpse of the creatures. This image snapped him out of his paralysis. They had a humanoid form, but their faces... their faces were anything but that of humans. They looked burnt up, with every other inch of their bodies being covered by what looked like dark robes that crept all the way to the ground. Their eyes were the worst. Nothing but darkness, and they covered half of the face, and at the bottom of said faces, two rows of teeth could be seen. These weren't normal teeth; they looked more like knives. He suddenly felt the urge to puke, but then he noticed that the sudden light rendered the two creatures blind for a second. Noticing this he threw his wallet at the opposite corner of the room and darted out through the door. The creatures immediately jumped at the corner where the sound came from, but before they knew it, the man was gone.

It was a long hall, stretching for what seemed to be miles. He had never been much of a runner, but because of what he had just seen, he couldn't help but run. His feet started to swell up and his stomach was signaling that he needed to stop, but he didn't. Any step in any direction opposite of the creatures was worth it, and he knew it. He ran, and ran, and ran, until he eventually fell on his knees. Sweat was dripping down his face. His feet felt like he'd been running on glass that whole time. His breath was so chaotic that he ended up puking right then and there. After he wiped his face he managed to get back up and walk some more. Before he knew it, he saw a light in the distance. It was far, farther than how far he ran up until then, but there definitely was something there. Before he could turn around to run away from it, he heard something, a voice. That humming... it was so familiar that he immediately felt tears running down his cheeks. It was his wife. He didn't know her name, didn't even remember what she looked like, but he knew, without a doubt, that it was her. Immediately after hearing that he started walking towards the light.

He walked, and he walked and he walked, until he couldn't even feel his legs anymore, but that didn't stop him. He had a goal now, a purpose. He was no longer running in the dark, he was running towards something. After a while he could feel his legs again, which was a bad sign. Pain had started to settle in once again, but the light... the light was getting closer and closer. It felt like years, walking towards a light and a simple humming sound, but eventually he caught up to them. It was a room so bright that he couldn't even look into it at first, but after a few seconds his eyes had adjusted to the sight, and what a sight it was. His wife, his beautiful wife was standing in the middle, humming to his two year old girl and his 4 year old son. Tears were running down like a waterfall on his face. He fell to his knees and started crawling towards them, when all of a sudden the humming stopped. This made him step back for a second.

"It... It's me!" he said, while gasping for air. "You... You remember me... right?"

The figures were all staring back at him now. The pressure broke down the last bit of sanity he had in him.

"It's me! Of course it's me! And you're my wife, my beautiful wife. And here's Jacob and Samara!" he screamed in an effort to break the silence.

"You don't remember, do you?" asked the woman, with a serious tone.

"Remember what? Doesn't matter what I remember and whatnot, what matters is the fact that we have to get the hell away before they come here."

She stared him down for a couple more seconds, then she picked up the two children and started walking in the opposite direction. After seeing that, he immediately got right back up and grabbed her arm.

"What the hell are you doing? We have to get out of here. Now, listen to me, there's something going on here and we need to get out as soon as possible or els-"he said right before he got interrupted by her slapping his hand away.

"We need to wait patiently to arrive. You really don't remember do you?" she said, with a look of pure hatred in her eyes.

"Remember what?" he shouted as loudly as he could. "Tell me, or else!" he clenched his fists.

She started laughing loudly; to the point where he couldn't help but step back to process what was happening.

"Remember why you are here, why we're all here. Remember what you did." She said, while continuing to laugh.

Before he could respond, he noticed that she was pointing to a desk nearby. He threw himself at the desk hoping to find answers. There was nothing on it, so he decided to open up the drawers. He was frantically throwing out everything inside until he found it. A photo album. He picked it up and started looking at every single picture until he reached one of the final pages. The picture on the left side of the album was a picture of him going inside the house carrying a bottle of liqueur. The picture on the right was his wife pushing him away from the children. He flipped the page and immediately dropped the whole album on the floor. There was blood everywhere, including on the paper that the photos were put in.

"Oh god... No... no no no..." he started shouting.

"Oh but yes," she said, while looking down at him. "You did this, you caused all of this" she said, while pointing down at another picture of him pulling the knife out of her. "I wasn't enough for you was I? You just had to finish the job right?" she flipped through the pages until she found the right one and threw it in his lap. The picture immediately made him puke whatever was left in him.

Before he could even react, he felt a set of hands grabbing his shoulders. The cackling was back, and he knew what was that grabbed him. But at that moment, all that he could do was accept it. The figures pulled him away from his family and back out the hall. They opened another set of doors before they eventually stopped and pushed him outside. There was nothing there. Nothing at all. Only darkness. The only thing that he could spot with his eyes was a sign that read "Welcome to your final destination, Hell".

STORY N. 3: 3 AM

"Dude, just give me a break already."

"You love her, you know you do."

"Dude, cut it out already."

"Excuse me for noticing the little fact that our friend has indeed, without a doubt, fallen for a pretty little angel."

"Dude I swear I'll punch you or something."

"Did you ask for her number yet or are you applying the psycho way to this like your last date?"

"Alright, you deserve this." He said as he punched his friend.

"Ew you touched me. That's like second hand cooties or something."

"One more word and I'll hit you again, Jeff."

"Oh no, we're using first names aren't we? Well fine then, Brody MacAllan, how do you like that huh?"

"Guys cut it out already, we're almost there."

"Shut up Steve. You're like the backup dancer of this circle. Always good for décor"

After joking around some more, the three ended up getting to their destination, the Ohio State University. They walked and they walked until they eventually stumbled upon the dorm.

Several hours had passed since then and they were all getting ready for bed. They've known each other for a good couple of years now, although, with this being their first year of college, they were obviously a bit nervous regardless. They messed around for a good couple more hours until they couldn't help but fall right to bed.

"Dude, this is crazy."

"Ugh, what is?"

"This whole place, can't you tell? It was refurbished so recently and yet it's so cheap to rent. Literally one of the cheapest options out there yet it looks like a 5 star hotel or something."

"What's your point?"

"My point is that I did my homework this time."

"This time... as opposed to any other time?"

"Shut up and listen dude. This place isn't what it looks like. Apparently a whole bunch of messed up stuff happened here. The type that is usually just swept under the rug for a cheaper price... you know what I'm saying right?"

"All that I know is that you've got to stop watching all of those late night horror movies dude. They're frying your brain or something."

"No dude, listen here. This used to be an orphanage way back and at the time when it was open twelve children went missing in the span of less than a year. And those are the only ones that were actually reported. This is why this was so cheap dude, they're trying to get people to stay here to make everyone forget about what –"

"Alright, that's enough. I never even heard of any orphanage being around anyway."

"That's because it was only active in the early 1900s dude, it's been just a castaway location until a few years back when they started working on it and now they're masking it as a dorm."

"Even if what you're saying is true we don't have anything to worry about. If there was some random child kidnapper at the time he's long gone by now. He'd be like what, over 140 years old? I'm pretty sure I can take on a 140 year old pervert. I'll protect your delicate skin, don't worry."

"All that I'm saying is that this doesn't sound alright... also, this place was run by nuns, not old men"

"Dude, you've always been obsessed with that sort of stuff. Just let it go already. There's no such thing as the supernatural. You're in college, enough fantasy and more trigonometry please."

"Fine, suit yourself. Don't come running to me when the ghost of the pedophile makes you wear a bonnet and a pink dress..."

Time seemed to slow down after this talk. Brody kept on dozing off and on again until he eventually heard a loud bang at the door. This immediately made him jump. It was only one bang but it was enough to make his heart jump out of his chest.

"G... guys... someone's at the door."

No answer. He tried again and again but his roommates were just sleeping without a care in the world. Before he could actually get up though, a familiar voice started talking from outside the door.

"Dude, let me in, please."

"J... Jeff? Is that you? What the hell are you doing outside at this late hour? How did you even manage to get yourself out there in the first place? Jesus you scared me half to death..." he said as he started wobbling towards the door.

"Let me in."

"Yeah, yeah I got you. Hold up for a second Jesus. Seriously though, how did you get yourself locked outside? I figured you at least had half a brain or something Jeff."

"What's your problem dude?" asked the same voice, only this time it didn't seem to come from the outside. It came from right behind him.

Startled at first, he immediately jumped to the side and fell on his back.

"What the hell dude I thought you were outside." He shouted loud enough to wake up their third roommate too.

"What's going on, why's everybody shouting?"

"Looks like Brody started sleepwalking or something. Seriously why would I be outside at this late hour, when the door's locked from the inside? Jesus, at least make a realistic nightmare or something."

"I swear it wasn't my imagination or anything. It was your voice. I heard it several times, asking me to let you in."

"Whatever you say, freakazoid, next time you hear it tell it to shut up and haunt your morning dreams or something. We've got to introduce ourselves tomorrow and I swear to God, if I end up with bags underneath my eyes I'm taking your laptop away and throwing it out into the trashcan."

"Alright, I'm sorry. Must have been the stress or something."

"Yeah, the stress. There you go. Now just go to sleep already dude."

After hashing things out, Brody and the rest ended up going back to bed. Despite the overall stressful situation that he just went through, Brody didn't seem to have a problem falling back asleep. That is, until a few hours later, when the voice came back.

"Let me in" said the voice.

"Not again... I swear, whoever's outside better cut this out before I get out there myself and bust you open with my baseball bat."

"Let me in, please" said the voice.

"Alright, you asked for it."

He got right back up, ready to put whoever was pulling the prank in a world of pain. He got up and immediately headed straight towards the baseball bat that was on the ground next to the kitchen table. He picked it up and went straight towards the desk where the keys were sitting on. He took them and started practically jogging towards the door.

The voice repeated itself, although this time it was different. It no longer sounded like his friend, Jeff, instead, it sounded exactly like his other roommate's voice, Steve.

"Let me in, please."

This made him freeze for a second, dropping the baseball bat on the ground. The noise made his roommates jump too, which was immediately followed by a loud groan from them.

"Are you serious dude? Like, are you for real right now?"

"I swear on everything that is holy, there's something outside and it seems to mimic your voices or something. I am not joking, I am not hallucinating, and I am not lying to you."

The two looked at each other and immediately jumped from their beds. Jeff went straight towards the kitchen, coming back only seconds after with a huge butcher's knife in his hand. Steve on the other hand went straight towards his trophy for winning first place in a swimming contest.

After they each gathered their own means of protecting themselves their burst right through the door, almost breaking its hinges while doing so. On the outside though there was nobody. Not a single person in sight. After inspecting for a couple more minutes the three went back inside.

"I swear guys, there was someone outside."

"Whatever dude. If you wake me up even one more time I swear to god I'll stab you."

"Yeah dude, seriously, what's gotten into you?"

"I'm so-"

He couldn't finish the sentence though because a sudden voice made them all freeze on the spot.

"Thank you for letting me in." Said the voice.

This time around though, it wasn't any of their voices, it didn't even sound human anymore. It resembled an old lady's voice and it sounded clear as day, but the location wasn't as easy to decipher. She seemed to be coming from everywhere around the room. The three immediately went back to back, looking around every possible corner trying to find the culprit of the sick prank.

Time seemed to slow down almost entirely. Everything went quiet until all of a sudden a loud bang made the three fall to their knees. The three sat there for a good couple of seconds before a second set of loud noises started spreading across the room. The beds started squeaking around while the books on the shelves were all falling straight down to the ground. The plates started crashing and spreading across the whole floor while the cups on the side started flinging across the room.

The three couldn't help but stand there, with petrified looks on their faces, staring at the spectacle happening right in front of them. That is, of course, until it all just seemed to stop, and the floor began to creek louder and louder, as if a very large person had just started walking around the room, getting closer and closer to them.

Jeff, being the eldest and most courageous among the three managed to pick himself up and immediately start swinging the knife around, hoping to graze the intruder and make them leave. No such luck though, as the knife seemed to hit nothing but air, until he felt a very sudden chest pain. He fell back to the ground, grasping for air as he started coughing up and rolling to his side.

The second to get up was Brody, but he didn't get up in order to fight back, quite the contrary actually. He ran straight towards Jeff, dodging the many different objects that were being thrown across the room after him. Before he could get to him though, he stepped right on a piece of broken glass, causing him to fall down to his knees too.

Steve on the other hand, after noticing what had happened to the two, immediately pulled out his crucifix and started saying a prayer. He prayed and prayed until all of a sudden the crucifix started heating up. He still tried holding onto it until he eventually couldn't help but throw it to the ground. Immediately after, the crucifix caught on fire, followed by another loud bang which made him cower underneath the bed.

He sat there, continuing to pray, until he heard the same voice call his name from behind him.

"Steve... Steve..." The voice whispered to his ears.

He closed his eyes, trying to avoid it, until he felt its hand on his neck, slowly grabbing a hold of it. Coldness, that's all that he felt afterwards. He could feel his life leaving his body, his eyes were sinking right into his skull and his mouth was gaping wide open gasping for air.

Jeff on the other hand started crawling to Brody, trying to push through the pain that made his heart beat right out of his chest. Tears started rolling over his cheeks and before he knew it he stopped moving altogether. He stood there for a good couple of seconds until he heard a familiar whimper coming from underneath the bed.

He noticed Steve's hand, trying to get ahold of literally anything he could which made him instantly push through the pain. He crawled and crawled, ignoring what felt like every bone in his body breaking, until he grabbed Steve's hand and started pulling him towards him.

After the two reconnected they immediately turned towards their friend, Brody, who had been whimpering on the ground for a couple of minutes now, pulling bits of broken glass out of his leg.

They started crawling towards him, slowly yet surely, inch by inch, but no matter how much they walked they still couldn't get to him. It was like something was keeping them in place, something was holding them back, not allowing them to proceed. They tried and they tried, until eventually they stopped altogether and decided on a different strategy.

"Brody!" shouted Jeff. "Brody can you hear me?"

"Brody come on already why can't you hear us!?" shouted Jeff.

But alas, no response came from their friend. It was almost as if he was in his own space, unlike the two of them.

"Ugh... what if... he's not really here... after all?"

"What do you mean?"

"Is that really... him?"

"Of course it's him, he's right there can't you see him?"

"I did not see him get back inside, did you? I saw you get inside, as we were shouting at him, but he never came back from the outside. He just sort of showed up at the same time as the voices, didn't he?"

"What are you saying? Is that... it?"

"Only one way to find out." Said Jeff while leaning back down in order to grab something from underneath the bed.

"What's that?"

"It's a cross I got from my grandparents. I've been carrying it around with me since they passed. It's good luck."

Right after he finished talking he started murmuring something to himself, and then he immediately started praying out loud. From the moment he started praying the air seemed to change, everything started feeling off. The air had become colder, so cold in fact that even their breath was visible at this time. This didn't stop him from praying though.

He prayed and he prayed, for a good couple of minutes, until objects started falling to the ground, noises stopped and everything calmed down. The only noise left was Brody's whimpering.

"Let's help him." Said Jeff.

"Are you crazy? I literally just told you that's not him. We need to escape out of this place before he turns around and munches out of your face or something."

"Dude, he's our friend. Let's give it a try, he's Brody I'm sure of it."

Jeff started walking towards Brody, Slowly yet surely, carefully handling a knife in his left hand. He leaned over to the crying man, patting him on the back.

"It's alright dude, it's alright. The worst has passed; we're getting out of here."

"Y...you didn't believe me then, did you?"

"I didn't, and I am sorry, but we've got to get out of here. Let's get you to a doctor or something."

"Oh god he's dead." He said, with a mortified look on his face.

"Who's dead?"

"Steve, I saw him get dragged underneath there and I heard his neck snap. Oh god it was horrible."

"What are you talking about? Steve's right –"

But before he could finish his sentence, he noticed the body underneath the bed. His eyes were rolled up into his head and his neck was twisted in such a way that it was a miracle it was even still clinging onto the rest of his body.

"Oh god, I just talked to him though, I swear I did."

"That... wasn't... him..."

All of a sudden it all started yet again. The ground was shaking, the dishes were flying all over the room, the air got cold yet again and the door flew right past them, going right through the window. Before they could react though, the beds collapsed over the two.

"You should have listened to me." Said the voice which now resembled the old woman again.

"What do you want from us?!" asked Jeff.

"I want to leave this place." It said, sounding more like a frightened child this time around.

"And if we take you, will you leave us alone?"

"Yes."

"We can't do that Jeff. If we do, we won't be the only ones suffering."

"We don't really have a choice, do we? I just want this to be over, man."

Their discussion was interrupted though by a very loud screech. It was Brody's voice, shouting at the top of his lungs.

"What's wrong?"

"My leg my leg my leg my leg!" he shouted repeatedly

What Jeff saw immediately made him vomit. His leg was splitting open, from the inside out. It was as if the creature was peeling it in half, as you would with a mere fruit. By the time it reached his knee the screaming was too much for Jeff to handle anymore, so he immediately shouted.

"Alright just let him go! I'll take you out!"

He immediately ran outside, but as he did that his hand held him back. Something was holding it; it felt as if his hand was simply put too big to even fit through the door anymore. The screaming returned soon after, with Brody's second leg being the one being split in half.

"Pull." Said the voice. "As if his life depends on it."

He pulled and he pulled, until it felt like his hand would break in half, and then he pulled some more. Nothing worked, no matter what angle he went for, no matter how much he tried, he couldn't get through it. At this point Brody wasn't even screaming anymore, it sounded more like he was just gargling and drowning in the mixture of blood, sweat and tears. That's when he knew that Brody didn't have much left. He had to try now, harder than ever before.

So, he pulled back, only to yank his hand as hard as he could. He was grinding his teeth, ignoring the massive pain that was coming from this action, yanking every couple of seconds despite not even being able to breathe anymore. He pulled and he pulled, until all of a sudden something happened. It... snapped.

His hand completely snapped, leaving him on his knees. What used to be his left arm was now nothing more than a bloody stub and with his knees resting carefully on the ground, he didn't feel the pain anymore, he only felt relief. Next to him lied a figure, a familiar one too.

"Thank you."

It was Steve, but at the same time it wasn't. It didn't matter to him anymore. He looked over to Brody, who was lying dead on his stomach. He looked like he had been dead for a couple of hours at least. As the figure started walking away into the dark hallway, Jeff felt his life leave his body. He fell on his stomach too, and with a last ditch effort, he started writing something with his own blood on the ground.

"It's not him."

STORY N. 4: Killer Claus

"Just... just give me more pills and let me go already."

"You know I can't do that. The reason as to why you are here in the first place is the betterment of yourself. I know this may come to you as a shock but I'm on your side here. So how about we go over this reoccurring nightmare of yours eh?"

"Fine. So it all began 3 months ago during Christmas. We got sent to a crime scene in a shopping mall. This was not your average crime scene though, it was a literal massacre. Eight people were brutally murdered; three of them were strangled to death while the rest were all limbless across the floor. At first we couldn't really see a pattern, except for the fact that all of the people that were killed were working at the same place, a Santa Claus meet-and-greet center."

"Ah yes, I seem to recall this on the news. It was quite the uproar considering the fact that these types of things don't usually happen in our small town. This must have made you feel right at home, right? I mean, a big time detective such as yourself must have seen a ton of stuff dozens of times more gruesome than this right?"

"Before I got transferred here it definitely wasn't easy, but I had the resources to get the answers that I needed. The problem with living in this quiet town is the fact that nobody is prepared to deal with any big-noisy town problems."

"I see. Please continue. I feel like this is how we can find the root of your problems. This might be painful to revisit but at the end of the day this is the best way to help you get over the trauma you experienced during that period of time."

"We checked every victim's ID but there really wasn't nothing there to connect them together. At first we figured this was your average psycho gone mad type of a scene, but the more we looked at everything around, the more elaborate and planned out it seemed. You see, this was a pretty busy shopping mall during arguably the most crowded period of the whole year, and yet nobody had seen anything. On top of that, all of the cameras had been turned off prior to the murders and the criminal even knew exactly in what order to take them all out before they could run out. The time of death is what bothered me the most though. Despite the fact that there was a wide opened door there that the victims could have escaped through they all seemed to die around 1 hour apart from one another. This means that the whole process took well over 8 hours. In such an enclosed space there is no possible way that this could have happened. It simply made no sense, especially since it seemed like 5 of them had been tortured quite brutally before being left to either bleed out on the floor or drown in their own blood."

"That is quite the conundrum, I have to agree. No wonder the case went unsolved for so long. It must have made you feel terribly small and powerless to see all of these horrific acts happen before you without being able to piece together everything."

"That's not all though."

"Oh? Do continue in that case."

"Why strangle the three people there? Why not cut them up like the rest? He still took an hour to kill each and every one of them, so why? Was the killer bored of doing the same thing? Did he want to feel something different this time around? Regardless it felt a lot more personal with the three than it felt with the other five, so I decided to run a background check on them and see what I could find."

"What do you mean more personal? Wouldn't cutting off people's limbs be the more personal method of taking them out?"

"In most cases yes, but in this case, they were all strangled for an hour each. They literally had their necks shattered with what seemed to be the work of a steel cord. This must have taken a very long time to do and it definitely felt more personal than the others. This also showcased the fact that the person knew what he was doing. This was definitely not the work of a newbie. Regardless though, after running a background check on those three people everything became a little clearer."

"Oh? I didn't hear about this on the news. From what I gathered, there was no link between the victims."

"Yeah, that's because I decided that there was no reason to throw away all of that information to the press. Wouldn't want the guy to know what we knew so I decided to take matters into my own hands and do a little research myself."

"Ah. Alright, go on then."

"So, what I noticed at first is that these three people, two guys in their late 40s and one woman in her early 30s were all pretty much just loners. They had no records of ever breaking the law either and were pretty upstanding citizens. That is, of course, until I found out something about the lady. Although she was quite the social outcast, she was known to be quite a frequent client at a local bar called The Rooster. She would pick up random dudes and hustle them out of a few drinks every now and then and of course, this made me wonder something else. What if she hooked up with the other two guys that were strangled? This took a lot of questioning, and it definitely wasn't easy. After all, asking the family of the victim that was killed if their daughter had plowed these two guys that were over 15 years older than her is not exactly something easy to do, but alas, my suspicions turned out to be true."

"Alright, so you found a connection between the three, but what about the other five?"

"This was the tricky part. You see, their families didn't know anyone else from the slaughter. Nobody knew anything about anyone else around there. They lived completely different lives, until that very moment. So, what if this was just a spur of the moment incident for the other five? What if the five just so happened to be in the way? What if the guy we're looking for was someone that hooked up with the girl, found out about the other two, decided to go at them and just didn't want any witnesses? No no no no. There still weren't enough pieces to completely finish up this puzzle. So, I decided that the legal ways weren't really getting me anywhere so I decided to do a little extracurricular research on my own."

"This is a safe area, no information gets out of my sessions, so you can go on if you're feeling comfortable with sharing this bit of info."

"Alright, so as I mentioned before, these people were basically just loners, they were your average outcasts that wouldn't really go out unless they absolutely had to, so I figured they must have had some anxiety issues and quite possibly that they might have been depressed at the time. This is when I decided to go back to their houses during nighttime and do a little digging myself. After taking a few DNA swabs and digging around some more I found the answer to my questions. I found a bottle of what seemed to be home-made anti-depressants.

"Those are quite illegal from what I know. Any idea where the person could have gotten them from? Also what do they have to do with the incident at hand?"

"I didn't know exactly at the time either, until I analyzed the contents of the pills and you won't believe this. There was an unhealthy amount of something called a Datura root in every capsule."

"Ugh, excuse me, but could you explain what that is?"

"Oh it's quite simple really. It is one of the main ingredients in most poisons out there. It is quite deadly even in its natural form, but if you were to ingest it in extremely small dosages on a daily basis you'd notice a way different reaction. Basically put, it destroys your mental state, it completely makes you bonkers. There have been cases of people becoming extremely violent and unintelligible from consuming a single small dosage, so you can guess what reaction they would have to the stress of working in a new place while being subjected to that substance."

"So, what you're saying is that these three went completely mental on the other 5 workers? Shouldn't that be the end of that or is there more to this story? This still doesn't explain why the other five didn't just leave or why they weren't shouting for their lives as they were being butchered."

"After that I requested a blood report on the three and it was a match, there were clear signs that they had been drugged up hours before they were killed. After checking up on the other five though I noticed something interesting. They also had traces of Datura roots in their blood, although it was obvious that it was a much higher dosage than in the case of the other three, since their muscles were completely paralyzed when we got there. But that's not even the best part. You see, I had found all of my answers, except for one. Where did they get the fake pills from? That's when it all clicked for me. They were depressed loners, they definitely needed to have visited a psychiatrist at one point or another, so I looked and I looked and I looked desperately until I found one that had had sessions with all of them. Can you guess who it is?"

"I'm afraid that I don't underst..."

"It took me a while to get in here; after all, you do keep quite a low profile. After a little more digging it all became quite clear though. You drugged them up slowly yet surely, they were already in a pretty dark place so you took advantage of them and twisted them around to do your bidding for you. I love that little camera you have on the side by the way, mind if I check on your discussions with the others real quick?"

"I'm going to need a lawyer. I'm not saying anything anymore."

"Sure thing bud. I should let you know though that I already took those tapes from you a few days ago when I made my first appointment. You should keep your windows closed during nighttime, wouldn't want any creeps coming through there right? Also, those pills you've been giving me, I had those checked out too and guess what I found in them? You wouldn't believe the kind of stuff they put in anti-depressants nowadays."

"Y...you..."

"Oh and don't try anything funny. I called for backup 30 minutes ago so they should arrive any minute now. It's all over. You lost. Nice talking with you doc."

STORY N. 5: Seven Snapshots of Silverthorne, Colorado

When we first got to Colorado, I could not believe my eyes. The endless mountains and forests, the gorgeous highways going up on hills, exposing endless valleys with tiny houses and outlets. A modern location where you could find a vibrant night scene on the one hand, and beautiful nature that has not been disturbed for centuries on the other hand.

I took this photo while driving up to Frisco. If you look here, you can see the mountains partially covered by the shadow of the clouds. Down to the right, you can see the outlets. To the left, you can see the Lowe's parking lot. Beautiful area.

If I had known what was about to happen, I would have turned around and ran as far away and as fast as I could.

My husband said that if you wanted to bury a body, this would be the area to do it. "It's too remote and there are too many locations to hide a body here", he said. I nodded my head, not really listening. I had a lot on my mind.

In this photo, you can see me sitting in the bus, in one of the blue Summit Stage chairs, staring at my phone. I was upset because of work, as usual. I was still working fast food at that time and I was dealing with a boss who didn't like my ethnicity. Does reverse racism exist? I think it does. She had a problem with me and me alone, probably because I came from East Europe. Or because I was smarter? Whiter? Knew better English? Who knows. It doesn't matter now. She's five feet under right now, somewhere in the woods of Dillon so who really cares what she thought about me?

This photo shows my husband and I smiling in front of Lake Dillon. It was a pretty chilly day, which is why we're wearing our jackets. I had a friend who used to say that the weather in Dillon is bipolar: now it's windy and cold and rainy and five minutes later it's warm and so warm, you have to wear a T-shirt. He is wearing his handsome I-know-I'm-sexy smile and I love him. I can't stop staring at him. He must be feeling the same about me if he did what he did.

A few hours before taking this photo, we were at home, in our studio apartment. Our room was a mess. I was on the bed, crying my eyes out and cursing her out. I was having a nice day at work before she clocked in and ruined it. He looked at me with a pained look on his face and offered a solution for this: murder.

I laughed and then hugged him. It's not worth it, I said. She's not worth going to prison for.

This photo right here brings back a lot of memories of that day. It's a photo of a coworker and I having a beer after clocking out. The view behind us is of an endless valley. It was cold that day, I remember that much. The shadow of the clouds was slowly engulfing the valley underneath us.

I was pissed. I had just had a really bad day at work and I was trying to unwind before going home to my husband. I didn't want him to know I almost killed her at work because I was so angry with her. I didn't want him to see me upset again.

But I didn't. I went home and I told him all about it. He went quiet for a little bit and then turned towards me. His eyes spoke volumes. I knew what we would have to do.

This photo right here shows our car, a gorgeous Subaru Outback, the most popular car in Colorado. It's strong and it can handle all the difficult terrains in Colorado with ease. We had bought it not too long before this because it was one of the cheapest cars available to us. I had learned how to drive on a Subaru Outback so we were pretty confident about this.

That night, my husband and I got into the car. He started driving. He didn't say a word, but I knew what was going to happen. We were driving towards her place. We didn't account for the husband who was more than likely at home and for her child who was also there. We were driving in that direction with a shovel in the back and a bag. I didn't know what he had planned for her and frankly, I didn't want to know. There might have been a slight chance of me stopping this and I didn't want to do this.

This is it, this is when it happened, and this is the point where my life changed. My husband got out of the car, picked up something from the trunk and went straight in. After what felt like an eternity had passed, waiting alone in the car, a familiar voice started shouting. It was her.

She was running away, actually no, she was crawling away. She was bleeding out of her left foot, or what was left of it. She looked straight at my car and then at me, and after recognizing me she immediately started running while screaming my name.

She clutched my slightly opened window, continuously shouting my name. She looked straight into my eyes and from that moment on I knew what I had to do.

"Oh my God, are you okay?"

"Someone... someone just entered my house and started attacking me and my family. Harold's trying to hold him off but I don't think he can handle him. Oh god please call 911 he took my phone and-"

"Shh, it's all over now; don't worry about it, not one bit."

"T...thanks." She sighed in relief. "What are you even doing around here anyways? Don't you live like on the other side of the city-"

"Hunting. We are hunting."

"H...hunting? We? What do you mean by that?! You're scaring me."

"I'm not the one that you should be scared of." I said calmly, while pointing behind her.

Before she could turn around though and face whatever I pointed towards, she immediately fell to the ground because a heavy object had hit her behind the head. Before she passed out she must have seen that she was hit with her own husband's head. I found it hilarious, really.

We put her in the trunk and sped off. I never loved my husband like I loved him at that moment. He was and will always be my everything. We sped off, going into the sunset until we eventually reached it, the place where I used to work.

We strung her up like the pig she was and we tied her neck around the company's logo. When she woke up she attempted to escape, to no avail though. My hubby tied her up so well, I was so proud of him. When she woke up he was nice enough to give her the coffee she always likes to brag with, the slightly more expensive one that she always flaunts around the workplace.

He got her a hot cup and promptly poured it all over her head. The screeches she made me even happier than before. She deserved this. So afterwards we got an idea. She really liked flaunting how skinny she was at the beginning, but let's be honest here, she wasn't like supermodel skinny. So, how about we help her out real quick?

It's a wonderful plan, isn't it? So, we pulled the finest knifes we could find and we decided to not stain her expensive clothes. After we undressed her carefully we decided that I was the one that deserved to make the first cut.

At first I'm not going to lie, it was a bit scary, but I immediately imagined the time I cut my birthday cake, the one that my hubby prepared for me. So, I continued, making the cut bigger and bigger, getting as much fat out of the way as possible. I just knew she'd love this new look we're helping her achieve.

That's when my hubby decided to step in. "Her cheeks are a bit too plump, don't you think so, honey? She could definitely use a little snippet here and here" he said while pointing towards her bloodshot cheeks. "You're right, get those ugly things off."

He proceeded to grab the cheeks, to which our guest immediately started screeching even louder than before. "Yeah, that's the jackpot right there." I said to him. He pulled her cheeks as hard as she could, until they were almost about to snap on their own, and then he pulled out the knife and started cutting away, same way he'd cut the bread in the morning for eggs and toast. God, I love him so much.

After a good couple of minutes she passed out. Actually, I believe she died altogether, not that it would make any difference, really, since only minutes after we decided to deal the killing blow to the neck.

So, that's how it happened. This memo will most likely not get anywhere, it will be just your average text thrown in the police files' bin. But alas, I had to tell someone all about it. Right as I write this the police sirens are blaring outside. Hubby is waiting for me to finish with a gun in his hand. We'll do this quick. Only regret I have is not having spent more time with him. On the next page you can find our last picture together. Just look at how beautiful his smile is. It is to die for, definitely.

Goodbye. See you at the end of the tunnel

STORY N. 6: The Labyrinth

With time every memory of his life faded. He couldn't hold on to anything anymore, not the image of his wife, nor the image of his baby daughter, nothing. It all felt like a lifetime ago, and the worst part was that he couldn't even remember himself anymore. Who was he, what were his hobbies? What did he do on a warm summer day? Did he love his family? Did they love him? It all seemed foreign to him now. But alas, he came to grips with this feeling of being lost in the world. Every now and then the people in black suits would show up. They would clean him, leave food on the ground and make sure he didn't try to off himself. Every time he did anything out of the ordinary the walls would start spinning and he'd fall to the ground. This was his life now.

But that all changed when the doors suddenly opened up and a bunch of people entered the room. They were all wearing white coats, and they had the most sadistic smiles on their faces. They grabbed him and started tying him to a strange looking trolley. He was too out of it to actually put up a fight, so he just went with it. One of the figures leaned over to him, whispering in his ears.

"This is your chance Alpha. Your only chance. A lot of money is in on this, so let's not mess this up, alright bud?" the figure smiled. It wasn't a happy-go-lucky smile; the words didn't come out as encouragement either, they seemed more like a threat than anything else.

Before he could respond, the walls started spinning again, and before he knew it, he was out cold. He couldn't even dream anymore. He had no way to imagine anything but the cruel reality of being stuck in that dark room, so his dreams consisted of darkness and silence.

He woke up in another dark room, but he felt different. This wasn't the place he'd usually wake up in, not even close. There was grass on the ground that tickled his feet and there wasn't anything but the bed and the walls around him. The place was smaller, around 5 meters wide, a perfect cube, but before he could say anything about it, the whole place started shaking. All of a sudden, the walls started to separate and before he knew it his eyes were hit by a light so bright that it made him plant his face into the ground for a couple of minutes straight. He hadn't seen a light that bright in years, that was for sure. After spending a good ten minutes facing straight down, he finally picked up the courage to get back up on his feet, still covering his eyes with his palms. He was sweating profusely already. After his eyes started to adjust to the light he started to look around him once again. This was no longer a dark room he was trapped in, quite the opposite. Greenery everywhere, nothing but flowers and grass. On his left and his right there were two solid green walls filled with flowers. Upon closer inspection he noticed that behind that greenery was a solid wall that was keeping him from advancing. The walls were around 10 meters tall, and in front of him there was nothing but an open field. His little investigation of his surroundings was stopped by a loud beeping alarm on his hand. A clock had started counting down. 60 minutes left until something happens. Scared of what this might imply he began running ahead, trying to look for a way out.

After a good 45 minutes of looking around he finally realized what kind of place he was put in. A maze. With every turn he took, it felt like his sanity was breaking apart. Why would they do this to him? What was the point of this game? To see him die? Would they allow him to die? He would much rather run across these fields than be stuck in that room, for sure, so he didn't mind the change of scenery. After running for another 15 minutes the clock on his arm started ringing and all of a sudden a loud set of drums started playing in the distance. He then heard a voice calling to him from the other side of a wall.

He immediately pushed his ear towards the wall and started listening in on the message that the strange individual was giving him.

"Take these... and good luck." Said the voice.

Before he could reply, the stranger started throwing a couple of items over the wall. A lighter, a bottle of strange liquid, a water bottle and a short blade. After picking them all up and inspecting them up close, he went back to the wall and started calling out to the stranger again, but there was no response.

Whoever that was, they were gone, for good. After chugging the bottle of water, he started walking again. But before he could actually look into whatever the other strange bottle contained, he suddenly felt a vine grabbing his foot. His reflexes kicked in instantly and he turned around, cutting the thing in half. Before he could actually celebrate his victory though he was completely covered in them. Long, spiky vines were pulling his every limb apart. His arms felt like they'd rip clean off any minute now. With a last ditch effort he managed to cut the vines that were holding his legs. With his legs free, he managed to run away instantly, ripping the vines clean off. While running he eventually seemed to notice a pattern. Every few hundred meters or so he'd see a red flower that was pointing to a certain path. Taking it as a good sign, he started following them and before he knew it he found the source of the attacks. A huge flower was spreading its vines across every wall and at the center of it all, a red seed the size of a basketball.

"If this is a game then I'll follow the rules and win" he thought to himself, and immediately jumped towards the seed. On his way there he could feel his heart rate speeding up, but before that could take a toll on his body he managed to throw the bottle of strange liquid at the seed. He then pulled out the lighter and started to light the thing on fire. A loud screech followed, which made him cower on the grass. After a good fifteen minutes of nothing but loud screeches the drums were back. He looked at his clock once again, and just as he feared, the clock had started moving yet again. This time, he only had 30 minutes to get ready.

He was a little tired already after running for so long, and with his adrenaline gone, he started to feel the pain from the vine attack. The spikes had left his whole body filled with open gash wounds. He tried ripping his clothes off and covering the cuts up, but there were too many for him to actually cover up completely, so he decided to ignore them for now. He walked for a good couple of minutes before noticing that there were no turns anymore, just a straight path. After a couple more minutes of walking he spotted a door that had writing on it.

It read: Here lies your second prize

Alongside a creature that you'll despise

It seeks to hunt, rip, cauterize

But pay attention to its eyes

Follow the path of its dreadful cries,

Cause that's where it'll meet its demise.

Don't be fooled by the creature's lies

For that's where truly hell resides

Just listen carefully for the flies,

For that's where you'll see past its guise.

He took a deep breath opened the door. The hallway was poorly lit by a single light. He already hated this place because it reminded him of his solitude in the empty dark room, but before he could turn back, the door shut behind him, leaving him no choice but to advance. After walking for a few more minutes he eventually found his prize, a pair of scissors. Desperation started hitting him. He started looking left and right, trying to figure this puzzle out, until it happened. His clock started ringing yet again. 30 minutes had passed and he already knew what that meant.

A few minutes later he started hearing a faint cry in the distance. It sounded like a toddler, but there was something different about it, something sinister. It almost sounded like someone doing a very good impression of a baby's cry. It sounded too fake. He walked and walked until he eventually caught up to the sound. It was an empty dark room. No light dared enter this room. The sound was clearly coming from inside. He braced himself and entered. The ground felt... different. It was full of bumps and holes, and the sound seemed to come from everywhere once he had started to walk in. Then he saw it. A little girl, crying in a corner. Its face was completely covered with hair. After bracing himself yet again, he decided to run straight towards it, but the moment he pulled out the scissors the crying stopped.

In a matter of seconds the whole ground started shaking, and then he realized it. That wasn't the ground; it was the creature's hair. Suddenly he fell on his back, right on the biggest wound he had. Blood started spurting out of it because of the pressure. He jumped right back on his feet, hoping he could muster enough adrenaline to ignore the wound yet again, but the combination of sweat, blood and mud made it impossible to ignore anymore. The creature was now standing up laughing at the intruder. The sounds it made almost sounded normal, but again, there was something strange about it. He rushed the creature and immediately punctured its chest with the scissors. Nothing. The only difference was the fact that the somewhat normal sounding laughter suddenly turned into a full out crazed howling. The laughter was so loud that he couldn't help but cover his ears. Suddenly he felt like his head was about to burst. Blood started pouring out of his ears and his eyes, making him fall right back down on his knees. The blood immediately got swallowed by the hair on the ground. This was a nightmare, it was too much. He could barely even hold the scissors in his hands anymore. With every passing second he lost more and more blood. His wounds weren't even a problem to him anymore because he knew that in a matter of minutes he'd be completely dry.

In a last ditch effort to live he decided to take the scissors and stab his own knee. The impulse immediately made him jump out of pain, but as soon as he was back up on his feet he aimed directly towards the creature's face. He grabbed as much hair as he could and pulled it towards him, exposing the creatures face. It was distorted, unlike anything he'd ever seen before in his life. It had a small mouth at the bottom of its face, and what seemed to be dozens of small red eyeballs that were staring him down. The more he looked at it, the more disgusting it seemed. Before he could get second thoughts though he started shouting right back at the thing and without a second of hesitation he ended up stabbing it multiple times in the eyes, making sure none of them were left untouched.

The laughter turned into a high pitch screech that lasted for a good couple of seconds, but eventually it stopped. The hair around him started to cover the body up, until it turned into a small black cocoon.

He had to crawl himself out of there. There was nothing he could do anymore except crawl. He crawled and he crawled, until eventually collapsing on the ground. A few moments later he heard his clock ring yet again. 10 minutes this time. He laughed, knowing he wasn't going to make it until the 10 minute mark, until he heard a door right next to him open. He crawled yet again towards it, hoping for some miracle cure that could help him escape this place. Once he entered it though, he saw it. A huge room filled with nothing but a bloody crowbar and a set of small bloody fingerprints on the ground.

The moment he spotted this scenery a loud voice started screaming through the walls.

"You did it you did it you did it you did it yo-"

The voice repeated the same couple of words over and over again. The more time passed, the faster the voice got and the more distorted the place became. Suddenly he noticed a figure standing in the background. It was a woman holding a bleeding baby in its arms.

"Whyyyy?!" The figure shouted, with a dreadful screech following its question.

Before he could cover his ears he heard dogs behind him. The growls the forced him to turn around and brace for their attacks, but as soon as he turned, he saw an image that will haunt him for the rest of his life. They weren't going for him; they were eating something, right there, in front of him. The cracking of the bones, the muffled screams and the growls of the beasts made tears run down his cheeks. He knew what they were eating and it completely horrified him. Behind him, the woman had gotten closer, she was right behind him now, asking the same question but louder and louder. The baby in her arms started convulsing and before he could even say a single word the woman started screeching louder than ever before. Because of how much blood he had already lost, all that he could do was stand there and witness everything. He couldn't move or shelter his eyes anymore.

A thousand questions started filling his mind up, and as he desperately tried to make sense of everything that was going on, he started remembering the poem that he read on the door. In order to kill the other creature he didn't need to focus on anything but its eyes, which meant...

And so, he tried to cover up every sound in the room, trying to focus on the sound of flies. After a few seconds, he eventually managed to pinpoint where the sound was coming from. It was coming from the rightmost corner of the room. He had no more blood to spill, no more reason to go on, but for some reason he couldn't stop there. He had to make this stop. He continued crawling, ignoring the events that were unfolding around him. The floor was drenched in his blood now; to the point where he didn't even feel anything anymore. He crawled and crawled, until he eventually arrived to the corner where the sound was coming from.

That's where he saw it. A switch covered in flies. Without a moment of hesitation he started pulling it down. The moment he did so, the screams stopped, the growling was no more, and the voices were gone. He sat there, in his own pool of blood, waiting for the sweet release of death, but before he could pass on he heard the doors open once again. This time though, the whole room lit up. There were people all around him celebrating each other. They were all wearing white coats. A familiar individual walked up to him and kneeled over to him to look him straight in the eyes.

"You did good. Congrats, you made it to the end. Now, you can rest."

Right after he finished his sentence he lifted the glass of wine he had in his hand and patted him on the back. The last words he could hear before he passed on were "Bring the next one over."

SCARY STORIES: VOL.3

STORY N. 1: The Killer

"Aahhhhh . . . !"

A blood-curdling scream penetrated the usual calm of the small town that was located in the middle of nowhere. Chaos accompanied the frenzied sound. Alarmed, people began rushing towards the source, which turned out to be Mrs. Mackenzie, the wise, old widow of the town's previous mayor. She was a headstrong woman with high morals, and she always seemed to have a smile for everyone. But she wasn't smiling now. Her face was contorted in terror and panic, making her bulging, almond-shaped eyes look almost too big for her face. Looking ashen, she covered her gaping mouth with one shaking hand. Gulping, she gingerly lifted the other hand to point at the narrow alley and looked me in the eyes. Her eyes, worse than her trembling body, were laced with fear: true fear, in every inch of them.

Understanding the gravity of the situation, I darted towards her. Just as I reached her side, she collapsed into my waiting arms. The gruesome scene in front of us amazed and frightened me. How could anyone be so cruel? What had the poor girl done to be brutally murdered? While I was indulging in my reverie, Jack, the local blacksmith, shuffled towards the mutilated body. Yet, the nauseating sight and the awful smell churned his stomach, so he began heading in my direction. He locked his jade eyes with my cobalt-blue ones, a silent message passing between us. He knelt down by my side and eased Mrs. Mackenzie out of my arms and into his. Knowing the plan, I made my way to the mangled mess in the pool of crimson blood.

The victim's disjointed legs and arms came into my periphery vision, and I inched as close as possible as I could, before the metallic scent of blood could overwhelm me. The girl lay on her back with her abdomen completely cut open. Slimy, pinkish and gray organs spilled out at him, and apparently, the murderer hadn't even spared her organs. Both her kidneys had been stabbed by a sharp knife multiple times, as indicated by their battered state. The organs encompassed the entire length of the abdomen, but some of them looked to be out of place. Her gall bladder was higher than it should have been, if I were remembering the huge body organs chart that I had to learn by heart in high school correctly. Something—I think it was the intestines—had been uncoiled and spread out evenly to cover the empty spaces. This meant a few of the organs had been removed from the body.

As I raised my head, something besides the body caught my eye. A small fist-sized chunk of red meat was wedged in between two slightly larger, tongue-pink swabs of meat. Suddenly, I realized that I was staring at the heart—jammed in between the lungs; just like how they were arranged in a body: but not inside this one. Disgusted with all the blood and body organs that lay on the pavement, I focused my gaze on the victim's head. Blood crusted the side of her right temple, as if she had been flung to the ground. Other than this gash, her face was injury-free, and she looked content; not even one crease marred the perpetual calm her face was exhibiting. Her countenance was not in tandem with the savagery committed to her body; weirdly, the openly presented peace on her face spooked me even more than the state of her body. What had she died thinking of? Didn't it scare or shock her to be murdered in such an inhuman way?

Constant chatter broke through my musings, and I decided to check how far the news had spread. Turning my back to the body, I saw that almost all the town's folks had stationed themselves at the edge of the alley. Horror, indignation, and repulsion was etched on most of their faces, and a woman sat wailing near the entrance of the alley—probably the dead girl's mother. Standing beside the sobbing mother, the sheriff and the imposing detective (who had been hired from the big city) shot me irked glances, mingled with begrudging respect. They both hated me, because I always ended up stumbling upon the crime scenes and appraised the damage before they even got there. Since my deductions managed to come awfully close to the real testimonies, they sometimes asked me to help them, even though it annoyed both of them—especially the sheriff.

Eyeing me as if I were a six-day-old rotten apple, the sheriff stalked off to bark orders at the paramedic staff, who had swarmed the alley just as I walked away from the body.

Detective Hamilton, on the other hand, stood ramrod straight, with his hands clenched at his side, kind of like how cadets in the military were taught to stand. Many of the locals were interested in his past, but none were bold enough to go toe-to-toe with his intimidating profile. On one occasion, I ventured to inquire about his career. Surprisingly, he was forthright in his reply, however, the brevity of his answers did not satisfy the researcher in me.

At present, he was observing me with a bemused expression, as if he could sense the direction of my thoughts. This was one other reason why the detective came off as domineering: he appeared to know what was running in the other person's mind and his hunches had allowed the town police department to trace a lot of criminals. To lighten the taunt tension in the air, he broke the ice first with his loud, guff voice.

"Mr. Reporter, you just studied the crime scene and the state of the body. Do you think the victim was another target of the Surgeon serial killer?"

I took my time answering, since I knew that it would vex him to watch me ponder whether to give him my opinion or not. Petty as it was, this childish act displayed my defiance to the way people obliged him, by answering his every question as if it were a matter of life and death. He hated having his authority questioned, so I made it a habit to question it on a regular basis. Felling like I had prolonged the inevitable for as long as I could, I spoke my mind.

"Frankly speaking, it's most definitely his insignia. But I didn't spot any missing limbs on this one."

"Seriously, what's with you and the statistics of murder? Even seasoned policemen are grossed out by how psychopaths carry out their trade. Yet, you seem fascinated by the various ways in which murderers kill people." Levelling me with a glare filled with distaste, he rattled on.

"Detective, in my defence, I just want to comprehend why they are willing to go such lengths? And what do they think they will achieve by murdering people?" I replied with a shrug.

Heaving a sigh, he gave me a brisk nod and turned to join the medics who were leaving with the sheriff. Out of nowhere, the hubbub of the scene accelerated my pulse; my heart started to pound erratically. I needed to get away, before I did something that I would regret later on. Sometimes, I ended up doing things that could get me in trouble, and it all commenced with me feeling uneasy and hassled. With panic gripping my heart, I ran as if the hounds of hell were on my trial.

Later in the evening, we were all gathered in the sheriff's dimly lit office. "We", being primarily me, the sheriff, Detective Hamilton, and Dr Graham (the doctor who had performed the autopsy on the dead body). Our little town only had one clinic, so some of its doctors had been assigned to handle the dead bodies. Dr Graham was a tough nut and competent at cleaning up a mess—a mutilated body—to find evidence, so he had become the go-to doctor whenever the Surgeon Serial Killer struck. He was a reed-like, thirtysomething young man, who had a fetish for donning long shirts that reached the knee, rather than the standard size men wore. As we all settled in, the esteemed doctor began explaining his findings.

"It's the Surgeon Killer alright, no doubt about that. The precision of the cut and the butchered nature of the body point to only him. The only thing that appears to be different from his other victims is her limbs haven't been sliced off, but they are bruised to the point of some bone breakage." Abruptly, glancing up from the autopsy report, he asked, **"Geez, when will you catch this guy? He has already killed four other women including this one—"**

"Hey! Stop right there. Your job is to tell us what the body told you, not to nag us to solve the case. I suggest you stick to what your meant to do, and leave the killer to the professionals. Now, tell us something that we don't know for a change." The sheriff shot daggers him.

This case had caused a lot of problems for the local law authorities. For five months, they had been chasing the killer, but to no avail. He had managed to elude them at every crossroad. So now, whenever anyone threw out the question of the murderer's capture, the sheriff went all spitfire on the poor chap or lady. Eventually, the people stopped asking, unless they were capable of withstand his wrath.

Ignoring the sheriff's warning, Dr Graham continued with his speech. **"Sheriff, you've got to admit that this case has taken too long, and the brutal killings need to be stopped. People are getting scared. Heck, some have even packed up and left, while some are thinking about leaving."**

Another pointed glare encouraged the doctor to let it go, and he returned to the autopsy results. Then he described in painstaking detail the extent of the damage to each of the organs. At the end of his lecture, he commented:

"Anyway, the girl was poisoned with chloroform, so she probably didn't feel any pain. I don't know if the cruel bastard is scared of hearing his victim's screams, or if he's sympathetic to their pain."

"Doctor, if he were sympathetic to them, he wouldn't kill them this barbarically. Besides, he might have drugged them to prevent any witnesses. After all, the victim's screams could have alerted other people." Detective Hamilton pointed out.

"You have a point there, detective." I exclaimed. **"We have five victims on our hands that were done in by the same serial killer. I remember the sheriff telling me that you had narrowed down potential killers—so fire away."**

The sheriff was more than happy to heed my words, and he directed our attention to the white board that had been propped up on the wooden desk near the slim window. Almost every inch of it was engulfed in the reports and notes related to the case; the only empty slots were the ones where the pictures of the victims and the potential murders were pinned. The photos somewhat illustrated the vandalism the true killer had inflicted on the poor girls. Subsequently, he informed us that all the targeted women were blond and ranged from the twenties to late thirties, in terms of age. They were not connected to one another, moreover, some of them were from out of town.

"We have identified three potential names of our serial killer." Detective Hamilton cut in. **"Norris Dangerman, Phillip Manchester, and Sean Tulip. All three of them have shaky alibies when most of the murders happened—in the span of five months—if we were to count this month."**

"Thank you, detective, for taking my words from me. But I think I can take it from here." The sheriff drawled in his cowboy-like accent: the exasperation imminent in his eyes.

"I'll dispatch one unit each to observe the activities of each of these men. The detective and I'll oversee two of the units." His gaze shifted from the others to solely rest on me.

"And, you Mr. Reporter, can make yourself useful by going along with the one that will watch over Mr. Tulip, the local butcher. I ain't going near him: he gives me the creeps."

After snarling out his order, he looked me straight in the eyes, daring me to challenge it. He knew that we shared the same sentiments for Mr. Sean Tulip. I wasn't going to back down from a direct attack, even if a shudder had rolled down my shoulders when I heard his words. I nodded curtly, and then the discussion turned to the semantics of observing the three potential killers. Outside, night had spread its thick, velvety cloak, patiently waiting for the town to slowly fall asleep.

In the wee hours of the morning, I left my apartment to watch Sean Tulip. My unit would meet me at the Danny' Meat in two hours, well after dawn. Mr. Tulip was an early bird, so when I turned the corner leading to his shop, he was already chopping away at a thigh of a boar. Surreptitiously, I took in his features; he was a burly man with strong, muscled forearms and his face was scrunched up, as if he found his profession and surroundings less than adequate. I peeked at his workstation, and saw that he was done with the thigh. He had now begun to pluck the feathers of a chicken. He cut a gash into its neck, letting all the blood drain from its body, before slicing it into chunks. Mr. Tulip was notorious as being cold-hearted to the animals he slaughtered.

Being a man of action, I snuck into his shop via the back door. If any evidence were to be found, I would likely come upon it in his office. Creeping soundlessly, I crossed the living room to climb the stairs to his living quarters and office. His wife had once rambled on to anyone who would listen about how odd it was for a butcher to have an office, but her husband had one in one of the rooms upstairs. Prowling around a house full of sleeping occupants was a new and thrilling experience for me. In a jiffy, my senses had sharpened, as I entered the house. Even a small creak would cause my heart to flutter in expectation and anxiety. With muffled footsteps, I crept to the first door on my right and gingerly turned the doorknob. One look inside confirmed that I had reached my destination.

After inspecting the littered papers, the dusty racks, and the unlocked drawers, I came to the solid conclusion that Mr. Tulip was indeed the Surgeon Serial Killer. Scattered amongst his own things in the drawers and racks, were the missing items of the victims: like a bracelet, scarf, or earring. Speed dialling the sheriff, I started walking downstairs. In my haste, I hadn't heard the sound of approaching footsteps, so when I reached the back door, Mr Tulip was face-to-face with me, a thunderous expression plastered on his grim face.

"Mind telling me what you're doing inside of my house again?" He growled.

Before I could come up with a plausible excuse, the front door burst open to reveal the lean form of the sheriff, accompanied by Detective Hamilton. Aghast and flabbergasted, the butcher looked from me to the unexpected visitors. Tongue-tied, he continued to stare at us incredulously, while I explained my finding to both of them. To cross-check my statement, they both darted up the stairs. Alas, they woke up the butcher's entire family since they weren't as silent as I had been. To say that Mr. Tulip's wife was dumbfounded was an understatement. When the sheriff hand cuffed her husband and charged him of the multiple murders, she went ballistic.

"How dare you accuse Sean of those heinous murders? He may butcher animals for a living, but he would never, ever kill a human being: you hear me? I demand you release him at once."

She would have taken a frying pan to the sheriff's head if Mr. Tulip hadn't calmed her down. In the face of his solemn judgement, she only sighed and earnestly promised us that we would see the error of our ways and let go of her husband. Later in the day, after locking up Mr. Tulip, we all went for a drink to celebrate the resolution of a long, hard case. Everyone was grinning from ear to ear, except Detective Hamilton. A crease had taken permanent residence on his forehead and his brows were perched high atop his head in a worrying frown. Bearing it no longer, he spilled his guts to us:

"Don't you guys think it was too easy? Surely, Mr. Tulip won't be stupid enough to place potential evidence against him in his own things if he really were the killer. It seems absurd."

"Are you saying what I think you're saying? You think he was framed." I gasped, my heartbeat picking up.

The sheriff grunted. **"Leave it, we've successfully closed the case. No point in second guessing."**

Before they could get into an argument over it, I bid them good-bye and took my leave from the bar. Outside, the blue sky, edged with scarlet and purple marked the beginning of a crisp evening with a slightly frigid breeze. My grey overcoat would protect my body, but my uncovered head was less fortunate. Huffing a deep breath, I stepped out into the cold evening air. The streets had more hordes than usual; evidently, the news of the murderer's capture had spread like wildfire through a forest. Feeling the urge to get away from the six or seven folks in front of me, I quickened my paces. As I was walking across a deserted neighbourhood, my eyes caught sight of her. She was rare beauty, with unruly blond curls, baby-blue eyes shaped like almonds, and she was dressed in a drab shirt and pants—but even they could not shadow her enthralling beauty. She reminded me of my mother: a woman who cared more about bewitching men than taking care of her own child.

Just then, as if he had been one with the background, I saw him. Slow and silent, like death, he was closing in on her with a razor-sharp knife clenched in one hand. As he approached her, the world grew eerily silent: like it was holding its breath for what was about to happen next. With his gray coat slashing against the evening breeze, he caught her waist and pinned her to his side. An uncanny scream resonated in the air. Panic-stricken, her trembling hand curled around the tip that was protruding out of her stomach. Deep red liquid soaked her clothes as she tried to struggle free. Plucking up the courage, she had even attempted to overpower him but failed, as she was too weak from the copious blood flow.

Jeering, he twisted the knife further into her abdomen. Yelping with pain, she took deep breaths to calm herself enough to think. I could see that she was brave, however, he was too powerful for her petite body to handle. Ruthlessly, he jerked the weapon out of her body and nailed her to the granite ground before she even had a chance to blink. Unbuttoning her shirt, he leered at her well-structured body and set the tip of his knife atop the centre of her collarbone. He greedily absorbed the ashen colour her face had taken, horror clearly evident on it. Without further ado, he sliced her till his knife rested against her lower stomach, just above her naval. Blood flowed out in rivulets down her sides and her pupils had long ago rolled up into her head. She was now as good as dead. Gutting her organs, he destroyed her body to his satisfaction. By the end of the whole spine-chilling process, her body looked even worse than his last victim's. He then advanced to remove her heart and lungs and placed them on the pavement to make his emblem.

While he mutilated her body, I just stood there, having long given up on trying to stop him when he appeared. He would never heed my commands to stop, but would blank me out of his mind. I am the only one who can put an end to these cruelties, but even I lose to his spirit that craves vengeance with a fierce intensity. To quench his bloodlust, he will murder and lacerate every girl or woman who remotely resembles our mother. My hatred for her matched his own, but I am supposed to be the good one, so I must make him cease these demonic acts before they devour us whole. We share the same mind, the same body. Yet, we are two jaded pieces of one soul. I am the killer.

STORY N. 2: And the Walls Echoed

Perched at the edge of the sheer cliff, the mansion's east wall overlooked a deathly drop seventy-five meters below to the tumultuous ocean. It was a historic and grand square-shaped mansion; it's towers in each of the four corners were architected in medieval castle style. The only moderation was the massive clock tower, erected in the centre of the courtyard, its dome hinting at Asian designs. Against the scarlet sky, it stood thundering and menacing at the bystanders who gawked at it. Lucy, the granddaughter of mansion's recently deceased owner, stood among them, gazing forlornly at her childhood home. Laying her eyes on the mansion had hit the truth home: she was back. This place held too many ill memories to ever deserve her love, and now she had been forced back due to grandfather's death and the issue with the inheritance. Straightening her spine, she plucked up her courage to face the music.

Her grandfather lay in his casket silently, his sharp and broad features and withering, white hair were just as she remembered them. Stiffening muscles indicated that rigor mortis had already set in. He had been dead for a while now. If Aunt Augusta's rambling were deciphered correctly, the old man had died somewhere around 3:00 am in the morning. However, due to the unusually wide divergence of his kin, the funeral had been scheduled for 4:00 pm at the latest. As Lucy took in his rigid form, the reality of the situation hit her briskly and unexpectedly. Even now, her love for him was pure, despite the cruelties he had allowed with his unrelenting silence.

Before she knew it, the funeral was over and Martha, the housekeeper, was whisking her away from the gathered crowd to the warm, isolated kitchen. She had been feeling faint and woozy there with her relatives watching he calculatingly—like vultures sizing up their prey. Martha must have picked up on her distress, as she often did when she was young. Lost in the strange, illegible whispers that were emanating from the walls of the kitchen, Lucy sank further into the cushioned seat. She sat there in an odd daze until Brandon came alongside Martha to collect her.

"I fixed one room for the both of you." Seeing Lucy's blank face, she quickly added. "Since the two of you are dating, I thought you might appreciate a bit of privacy."

At her words, Lucy shook her head slightly, but Brendon had already covered up her mistake by delighting Martha with a dazzling smile and guided Lucy to their room. Brendon was not her boyfriend, but in fact, a bodyguard her mother had employed to protect her at the mansion. Her mother didn't trust anyone in the mansion to keep her safe. When Lucy protested, her mother made her recall the nasty and petrifying incidents that had happened to her there before. Every summer, when she came to stay, dead crows would be left in front of her room and dangerous insects would be sneaked into her meals occasionally.

But these weren't the cases that worried her mother the most. When she was thirteen, she had gone alone to visit her grandparents, as her deadbeat of a father had divorced her mother when she was seven. During that visit, nothing frightening occurred, until the last day of her visit. She had been trapped by someone or something in the basement, in the abandoned western wing of the enormous mansion. It was the spookiest room in the entire place: it steel walls crusted with dried blood and scraped with lines depicting the time trackers prisoners made in their prison rooms. It was a daunting place—better left locked up. Lucy's mind was whirling with the memories from her childhood before sleep claimed her.

Howling in agony and terror, Lucy jerked awake to find herself peering into Brendon's concerned, aqua-blue eyes. Reflected in those eyes was a bedraggled girl, her breathing ragged, her clothes glued to her body with sweat, and her eyes filled with primal fear. Sobs begun to wrack her body; fat water droplets rolled down into the sheets beneath her, and she grasped his hand tightly, never wanting to let go. *They* had been consistently whispering to her and showing her horrible things while she had slept. Even now when she was awake, the whispers hadn't ceased. Instead, it seemed as if they had picked up with a fervor.

"We shall destroy you and your kin. You have wronged us, kin of Brad, made us suffer and held us prisoners in this godforsaken place . . ."

"Vengeance shall be ours!!!"

"Help us! Please, you are our only hope."

The voices reeled on. Their words had evoked a deep fear and longing inside her. When she asked Brendon if he could hear them too, he shook his head in confusion. What was going on here? Was the mansion haunted? And then, there was her dream. In it, she had been walking towards something or someone in a room, splashed with fresh blood, its metallic smell still lurking in her nose. Before she could discuss it with Brendon, a spectral screech made her bolt to the hall, with her bodyguard hot on her heels. Abruptly, Lucy pushed open Melissa's door to see what had happened.

Melissa sat onto her bed, a quilt wrapped around her legs, her body quaking and her eyes bulging with terror. Instantaneously, Lucy rushed to her side and took her hands.

"What do you see, Mel? Tell me, dear. It's alright," Lucy uttered evenly.

Melissa swiftly turned to face her cousin, stared at the vivid agitation in her eyes, and words suddenly tumbled out of her. She had sworn never to tell anyone about him, but there was something about Lucy that made her break her vow at that moment.

"He's behind the curtain."

"Who?" Lucy inquired softly.

"I don't know who he is, but he only shows himself to me sometime. His face is completely white, his black pupilless eyes are rimmed with red, and he wears a long, blue priest dress. He scars the heck out of me, Lucy. He—"

Lucy cut into her prattle: **"Slow down, Mel before your asthma kicks in."**

Gulping a few breaths, Mel pointed to where the nefarious creature stood. She then told them that she had been seeing him since she had come here—a week before. He had also been playing heinous pranks on her; a dead rodent in her bed, spiders in her brush sets (she hated those six-legged beasts), and he had even caused her mother to fall down the stairs. Melissa had tried to understand why he was hurting her and her family, but he never spoke of his reason and even if he spoke, she couldn't hear him. Her words settled deep inside Lucy, and she fiercely urged herself to look at the curtain where the demon stood. Brow furrowed in concentration, she perked up her ears. Ten minutes passed and she heard no sound. Sighing, Lucy was just about to give up when a sinister tirade caught her extra-sensitive ears.

"You are Luke's most treasured grandchild: the one who can hear our whispers. A truly magnificent power—but it won't save you or your wretched family from our wrath. A millennium—some of us have waited—to utterly destroy the clan that imprisoned us; and now with the last master dead, we can now bathe in their descendants' blood. We shall savour our revenge to the fullest."

Goosebumps broke out onto Lucy's skin as he let out a hair-raising laugh. It was a laugh of a lunatic; a lunatic who was out for blood. She couldn't bear more of his taunting insults, so she covered her ears with her hands. Her body was shaking with adrenaline, with her breath coming out in painful puffs. The whispering walls were closing in on her. Shutting her eyes, she tried desperately to escape into her mind. Out of the blue, she felt her back being rubbed in slow circles. It was soothing and appeared to be calming her erratic heart. When she opened her eyes, she saw that Brendon had taken charge of the situation, when her fright had gotten the better of her. Light-headed, she crept out of Melissa's room with Brendon's help.

At the crack of dawn, Luke Gateway's lawyer visited. At 6:00 am, Diana Gateway, his wife, had gathered all the members of her family that were at the mansion in her room. Her daughter Augusta sat on the chaise by the window, while her two grandchildren, Melissa and David—her dead sons' children—had flopped onto the couch as soon as they entered the room, whining about being woken up early. The last to arrive was Lucy, the child of her late oldest son. Out of breath, she hurried into the room with Brendon by her side. Irked at an outsider joining the family meeting, Augusta ordered him to leave. He didn't budge and looked over to Diana, the real authority in the room.

"He may stay," came Diana's placid reply.

When the newcomers had settled in, she began.

"As you lot know, my husband died last morning. Well, ever the caretaker he was, he has left a sizable fortune to all of you. However, the house is another matter altogether. The one among you who discovers what the family legacy is shall be its proud owner."

Aunt Augusta intervened. **"Wait, mother, isn't the house entitled to you?"**

"No child, it was never mine but his, and now it will go to one of his grandchildren."

David spoke up smartly, **"Grandmother, what do you mean by legacy?"**

"I'm talking about the bequest your grandfather's family has held for more than a millennium, you dimwit."

Lucy heard nothing after the word millennium. For her time had slowed down, thoughts were whirring in and out of her brain and a pounding headache was starting to muddle them. What did it mean? The demon had mentioned *millennium,* and grandfather's so-called legacy also dated back a thousand years. This couldn't be a coincidence, right? Or could it all be related as to why the malicious spirit wanted her grandfather's kin dead? Her grandmother was wise, so she might know. After everyone had drifted out of the room, Lucy saw her chance. She wished to be alone with the old woman, so she asked her bodyguard to run an errand for her. He gave her a pointed look but left anyway.

To say that the conversation with Diana Gateway was illuminating was an understatement. It was ghastly enlightening, in the best and the worst sense. She could hear the whispers; a demon was stalking Melissa, and David was blatantly clueless about the horror hidden in the walls of this magnificent mansion. To better comprehend her grandmother's cryptic words, Lucy found herself heading towards the locked basement. On her way there, she snagged the key from Martha's kitchen, where all the keys hung on a rack by the window. As she stood outside the towering door, Lucy couldn't comprehend why she was thinking of doing this. This place was a ghost-infested horror house.

Swallowing a lump in her throat, Lucy turned the key and shoved open the door to her impending doom. Trekking down the steps, Lucy rested her eyes on the floor of the basement. It was the same as always—dried blood everywhere. The fear enveloped her ruthlessly, as the events depicting when she had been trapped here before crossed her mind. She rubbed her chest frantically, trying to slow down her rupturing heart. Just as she had managed to relax herself a little, she heard their horrid whispers. She held her head high, ready to face them head on.

Visions. Blood-curdling visions were thrown at her. A knife being used on a babe and its cowering mother; two negros shot at while trying to escape this hell; a man's face laced with fear and pain while his perpetrator carved blood tattoos with a scalpel on his bare skin; dead bodies being raped and filled with harmful herbs in the name of science; a young man's face burning with acid thrown at it; and thousand more assaulted her. In all of them, the persons committing the horrendous deeds were men, and even some women, bearing resemblance to her family. They were her ancestors; this was their legacy. A legacy grandfather wanted them to get rid of once and for all, as indicated by grandmother's words. Her world spun on its axis, and her legs buckled under her weight at the revelation.

Melissa's demon sneered, **"You see now, girl: your clan has wronged us, humiliated and violated us in the most inhuman ways. They are dead to this world, so we cannot touch them, but you and your current family are another matter. Blood is blood: and we shall quench our insatiable thirst with your blood."**

"Why?"

"Got anything left to throw at us, little worm." Another voice reverberated.

"Why must we suffer when we didn't harm you? It's not fair." Lucy's petulant voice echoed through the enclosed space.

Gasps went all around the room and everyone started mumbling incoherently.

"Not fair, she says."

"The nerve of her."

"How dare she?"

"Silence!" The demon bellowed to the avalanche of voices. The voices fell away immediately, engulfing the room in a taut silence. To intimidate her, the demon materialised in front of her. Following his lead, the other ghosts also appeared before her. They looked remarkedly like how ghosts were supposed to look: wispy and unearthly, but even her untrained human eye could tell that they had taken their wounds to the grave. Skin peeling; gashes on the head; marks carved on skin; heart impaled with blades; and many other injuries were ingrained on their ghostly bodies. The demon was the most worse off; his face seemed to have been burned by acid or flames. Seeing them like this hit the point home, and she finally understood their vehement desire for revenge.

Still, she had to protect her family, who were ignorant of this dilemma. Her grandmother had remarked that Lucy and her cousins had been the lucky ones among the family. All of their fathers had died, so they had not been introduced and forced into the family's sordid legacy when they were children. With acid churning in the pit of her stomach, she shuddered out a request.

"T-There must be something that I can do. Please tell me what w-will make you stop."

Eyeing her pensively, a lady ghost took it upon her to argue Lucy's case with the others, while the demon vetoed all her suggestions. With malice and mischief tainting his eyes, Melissa's ghost dared Lucy to crush the divine stone that kept them imprisoned here. Some of the ghosts gaped in shock, but others joined the demon in his nefarious plan against her. Feeling ice cold, Lucy gave into his demands.

"Where will I find this stone?" Her quivering voice belied the brave face she had donned.

"Where it's always been, little girl." Then he spread out his arms to indicate the entire basement.

Scuffling away from him, Lucy began searching every nook and cranny of the jinxed place. As she was crouched on the floor, near the east side of the wall, her hand skimmed over something that send a jolt down her arm. She knew what she had to do; the consequences be dammed. With wavering lips, she recited after the lady ghost the incantations to fracture it. No one else had deigned to help, but the lady ghost had relented to her pleading eyes, and even warned her of the harm to her soul this ritual could inflict. Just as she was near its end, the door suddenly erupted open.

Without opening her eyes, Lucy knew that Melissa, David, and Brendon had bolted into the basement, disturbing the procedure slightly. Against the roaring in her ears, Lucy compelled her lips to move faster.

"What? Why are they all here?" Wailing madly, Melissa sank to the floor.

"Ghosts! So many of them. Lucy what have you done?"

Lucy fervently ignored her, and to get her attention, Melissa continued her ranting. When Lucy's casting was completed, a warm, white light engulfed the ghost and her. Slowly, the ghost started to disappear, finally free from this hell. As the last of the spirits left, Lucy fainted.

A month later, Diana Gateway lay in her bed, mourning the demise of her kindest grandchild. Lucy was still in her coma, and the doctors had given up a week prior. Everyone was utterly devastated. Even her mother had come to the house she swore she would never set foot into, because of her daughter's abysmal state. Lucy had always been Diana's favourite, with her natural charm, a steel backbone, and limitless compassion. Gazing forlornly at her late husband's portrait, she said:

"Please dear, I already lost you and I don't want to lose anyone else. Give me a sign if she alive, her coma is gradually killing me from the inside. Please, I beg you. Please." Tears leaking out, Diana sobbed into her hands.

Sometime that evening, when the family and guests were scattered in the drawing room, Melissa and her mother, Augusta, were watching TV. David was trying to finish his latest novel, Lucy's mother and grandmother were staring woefully at the sunset. Brendon was lost in his thoughts. A double knock caught their attention. They all turned towards the table to see the vase filled with pink-and-white Peonies. Instantly, Diana was on her feet. With wide eyes, she took in their splendid form and a tear streaked down her cheek.

"She alive. Lucy's alive!" She exclaimed uncontrollably, joy lightening up her features.

"How do you know, grandmother?" David looked at her like she might have gone mad.

"Boy, don't you know flowers at all? Peonies symbolise healing. She is healing and she will come back to us soon." Diana tutted him.

They had been given hope and now they would wait.

STORY N. 3: The Twins

Dark, ominous clouds lined the sky, threatening to send torrents of rain mingled with thunder and lightening to the house below. The house was a small two-story, with several arched windows and a patio. Ostensibly, it was just an average looking family villa, but in reality, it hid too many unsolved mysteries and deaths. Many ungodly rumours surrounded the elaborately decorated house at the end of the street. Women were said to have inexplicably disappeared there, cries of babies broke out in the middle of the night, only to be replaced by a deafening screeching sound in the next moment, and the ghost of a dead woman was said to hunt its hall. For the doughty kids in the neighbourhood, the house had become a source of fascination and mystery.

These rumours had instigated Mr Tom Delany, a meagre reporter from the *Daily News* (a local newspaper), to investigate the bizarre occurrences. He had been searching for an intriguing story to boost his position at the newspaper, and he thought this was it. It would be his big break if he played his cards right. He arrived at the fey villa sometime after noon and saw, to his surprise, four other people—two adults and two children—waiting for the landlord to open its crusted gates. To even the playing ground, Tom chatted with them for a while.

The gorgeous woman among them was Anna Yamamoto, a psychic who hosted a paranormal program on television. She had been requested by her colleague to prod out the real truth behind the house, as the studio wanted to do a show there. The blond-haired man was a priest, and he had come for his customary rounds to spot any irregularities. The house was such a horror spot that he had to visit it twice a week to appease the town's people. The children were twin girls named Gazelle and Arabella from the neighbourhood, who both religiously loved mysteries and ghost stories, so they had dropped by for a routine adventure. At around 3 pm, the gate promptly scraped open: no landlord in sight. This sent a shiver down Tom's spine, while Anna nodded absently and huffed out a breath of irritation.

"Such mediocre tricks that even a child can pull off. This place is a hoax, a prankster's favourite prank spot, and nothing more." She said, irked.

Studiously ignoring her opinion, we all let ourselves in, skimming over the mouldy spots in the dinning room, the warm coffee cup and emptied plates in the kitchen, and the odd, frightening lines drawn on the walls: as if to keep track of the time. Someone was living in this deteriorating house. This alarming revelation unsettled Tom and the priest, while Anna just appeared bored. Anna had seen too many ghastly things due to her powers, that such mundane things like breaking and entering seemed ordinary to her. During the time in which the three adults searched for the stranger, the twins both sat cross-legged on the floor, playing with voodoo dolls that looked exceedingly similar to the three adults who were prowling around the house.

A clapping sound near the front of the meandering maze spooked all of them, even clairvoyant Anna. The three adults sprinted towards it, their hearts pounding with panting breath mingling in the frosty air. When they reached their destination, they were astonished to see the twins with their ears glued to the wall from where the spine-shivering sounds were emanating from. Just as they had convinced the girls to step away from the wall, the baleful clapping stopped straight away. An eerie calm and silence enveloped the room, similar to the calm before a heinous storm. The tension in the air was as taut as the string of a kite soaring high in the blue skies.

Anna sensed a shift in the air that hadn't been there before. It felt as if something were getting ready to toy with them—make them its entertainment—and then it would throw them away in the worst possible way—death. The sudden thought, unexpected and unbidden, chilled her blood. This place was definitely not a joke; the entity that ruled it was menacing and blood thirsty. She had to communicate with it to fully understand it before it decided to launch an attack. Fingers tucked under her chin, she mused about what she would require for such a ritual.

On the couch, the twin's faces turned sour, as if they had seen something that did not sit well with them. Seething, Gazelle huffed out,

"She's getting too close. We need to get rid of her."

Arabella seconded her, **"I agree, she will become a nuisance if we don't stop her soon."**

As Anna plotted to restraint the entity, the twins' devised great plans.

Somehow or the other, Anna told her plan to communicate with the entity in the house to the reporter and the priest. But, the priest, better known to his peers as Father Norris (she had to pry his name out of him), took to her case and was merciless in his questions and critique. With the men's help, she had managed to clear the floor cluttered with strange items and had set up candles on the tables in the room. Sitting cross-legged on the ground, she beckoned the men to do the same and gestured for the twins to join them. Grinning with glee and something else that Anna could not identify, the girls settled onto the hard, cold floor. When everyone's eyes were closed, Anna began.

"Oh, holy spirits of God, guide us to the evil that lurks in this house. Aid us in understanding it and to lead it away from this dwelling. Safeguard—"

To see why Anna had stopped mid-way, her audience opened their eyes, only to be graced with a grisly view. Blood was gushing out of Anna's ribcage, her face rigid with pain. Apparently, a knife had been hurled from out of nowhere towards her during the ritual. Father Norris was on his feet in a nanosecond and eased Anna to the floor and into a sleeping position, while Tom scanned the room for pieces of clothing that they could use. Having found sufficient lumps of fabric, Tom bolted to Anna's side. With quaking hands, he attempted to stop the intensive blood flow. Picking up on his plan, the priest snagged a few cloths and stared putting pressure with them on her wound. Despite their best effort, Anna died. Her face had slackened, her limbs were becoming limp, and her eyes looked glassy and surreal.

Resigned, the men carried her stiffening body to the couch, closed her half-lidded eyes and covered her with a white cloth. Paying their respects to her, the men acknowledged that it was prudent leave this haunted house before things got even worse.

Anna had been too close to the truth and the ghosts of this ill-starred villa had passed her a death sentence due to her nosiness and naivete. She though she could run them out of their house; she was wrong, and she had paid the price for it.

Tom and the Priest gathered their things and hustled the twins out to the patio along with them. Nerves on end, they thought they would be able to breath a sigh of relief as soon as they crossed the gate to the outside world, but they were wrong. The gate appeared to be jammed in place, refusing to budge from its locked position. If it had been a small and tiny gate, the men might have hopped over to escape; alas it was very tall, with sharp spikes on its top curve. Shoulders slumping, they both retreated backwards, taking a minute to organize their perplexed and muffled thoughts.

"I am going to scout the area around the house. It might help us find an alternative escape route." The priest said to Tom.

Tom goggled at him like he was a lunatic and voiced his concerns: **"Are you sure? Being separated might make us into victims of whoever or whatever killed Miss Yamamoto."**

Pinning him with a glare, the priest stormed off towards the right side of the house. Tom pondered his options when he was left alone with the twins. With nothing coming to mind, he sat down with the girls and watched their antics with the voodoo dolls. They were stabbing pins into one that was clad in a priest-like robe and a blond strand of hair on its head tweaked Tom's brain. It looked peculiarly similar to the priest's hair. Voodoo dolls were often used in black magic to cause harm to people by just attaching a strand of their hair on its head. A tendril of dread made its way into his heart at this disturbing thought. Before he could dismiss it as a far-fetched theory, a shout echoed though the air.

It had sounded awfully like the priest's gravelly voice. Following the scream, Tom found the priest amidst a pool of crimson blood. His body appeared to have been sliced in half, horizontally from the stomach. Tom galloped back to the patio, his face ashen, his hands shaking unyieldingly and blood roaring in his ears. At the patio, Tom inadvertently turned to scrutinize the twins and the voodoo doll in their hands. They had ripped it in half—just like how the priest had been killed.

Catching notice of a petrified Tom and the horror etched onto his face, Gazelle let out a blood-curdling laugh.

"Look at him Arabella. He's found us out and can't believe his misfortune."

"Oh yes, what shall we do with him now? He knows." Arabella feigned her anxiety.

"Hmm. What shall we do, indeed?" Gazelle ogled him wolfishly.

Arabella suggested, **"We could eat him, or roast him, and then devour him whole. My mouth's watering just thinking about it."**

Raising her hand, Gazelle smirked evilly. **"No, I have got a better idea. He will spread our tale to the world."**

Before her twin could disagree, Gazelle explained in excruciating detail about their origin as two entities with vast magical prowess. She described the malevolent acts they had eagerly committed over the many centuries they had lived in the human realm. She weaved a terrifying story that made Tom shudder inwardly. To drive the point home further, the two entities transformed into horrendous demon spawns in front of him. Sprouting horns out of their head, they had vomit-green, scrunched up faces similar to snakes, abdomens of a scaly reptile and twisted feet—the toes of their feet adjacent to their backs and the sole adjacent to the front part of their bodies. Every inch of them screamed that they both were dammed beings—not for this world.

Finished with her monologue, Gazelle let Tom Delany jostle away to publish their story. If he didn't, an atrocious end would await him, just like it had all the other who ventured to cross the Witchling sisters.

STORY N. 4: The Halloween King

Del watched as the humans circled the room in packs, indulging in idle chitchat along the way. Despite the many years he had been living with them, humans were still an enigma to him. It was strange really; he was a human himself, but at times he thought of himself as being separate from them. Often, in the dead of night, he would hear their whispers. Forces that were unseen to the world of men would peek at him from the cover of darkness, taunting and laughing at him for reasons he didn't know. Even today, at the annual gala hosted by Mr. Mortimer in an abandoned mansion, he could hear inhuman sounds that no doubt belonged to otherworldly creatures. They were faint, muffled beyond comprehension, yet they were still there.

As a slight shudder rolled down his shoulders, he shook his head once to clear the wave of voices clashing against his ears and began mingling with his peers. Every year without fail, the boss of their small start-up company, Mr. Mortimer, would throw a gala to collect funds for some charity or the other, and every year he would choose this manor as the venue. It oozed out a spookily mystical aura, owning to its grayish, granite walls, paneled windows with the glass tainted blood-red. Bored with the monotone conversations whirling around in the hall, Del concluded it was late enough for a drink or two. When he snatched a champagne flute from a passing server, a shadow eclipsed his hand. Astounded, he almost let go of the flute. Regaining his balance, he tried to search for it again, even as his stomach dropped.

Relieved that the shadow had just been a figment of his imagination, Del swallowed the bubbly liquid in the curved glass in one sip. For a human, he had a remarkable tolerance for alcohol, and he usually drank one flute very quickly. Out of nowhere, he felt nauseated. Holding his rumbling stomach, he made his way to the outdoor garden to catch some fresh air. As the cool night breeze twirled Del's raven-black locks, his eye lids drooped. Leaning against the tree trunk, he tried desperately to shake off the drowsiness, but it was futile. Before he knew it, he was asleep.

The tangled branches of the willow tree above him furrowed sadly and decided to stand vigil over the sleeping creature. The time for them to come out was quickly approaching, so if he didn't guard this poor creature, the monsters of the night would take advantage of him. Sighing into the wind, the old willow spread out its roots to hide the creature from sight and prayed for the best.

The full, yellow moon marked the mid of the lunar calendar. The holy or demented day—it depended on who you are asking, the demons or the humans—was upon them. Today, they would raise hell in the manor they had been confined to by their tyrant master. Today, they would battle for power over the others. Today, they would parade the many human lives they had taken over the course of a year. Whoever won the competition today would become the left hand of the Halloween King, Zharagus. Old Willow's bone quaked just thinking about the boss of the demons. He had to protect the creature residing among his roots from them, or the prophecy would never be fulfilled.

Sometime after midnight, Del was roused from his slumber because of a constant hammering sound above him. He sat up, or tried to, but an unseen force jerked him back into a crouched position. He attempted hopelessly to kick the damp, staunch wooden roots binding him in place. He might as well have been pushing against an iron wall, with the way the roots wouldn't budge. Giving up on his struggle, Del strained his ears to pick up on what was happening around him. He heard chattering near him. Hurried voices, which sometimes bellowed suddenly with anger and slurred-over vowels.

"Where is he? I know you're hiding a human, Old Willow. Don't forget—one word to Zharagus, and you'll be burned to give us folks some warmth." A dry and throaty voice rasped out in fury at the person called Willow.

A painful lump started to gather in Del's throat when his ears caught a whiff of the scratchy voice. He wanted to break free of his chains to warn Willow to escape: the other person was his enemy. He would destroy him in cold blood without a second thought. Yet, most odd wasn't the fear Del felt, it was the train of memories that rushed into his brain at the moment when the voice infiltrated his brain.

He was peeking through a peephole into a lavishly decorated room: a stranger stood with his back to him, looking out the tainted-red window. He wore a long, cuffed black coat, whose hem rested against the stranger's shins. On closer inspection, Del saw that his bare legs were pearly white and arranged like bones. Just as his befuddled brain was processing this piece of information, the eerie stranger turned. Del gasped loudly. The stranger was a skeleton without any trinket of flesh. Monstrous-looking ribs peeked at Del from behind the stranger's see-through shirt. He should run while the bone man searched for the source of the gasp, yet his feet refused to obey him. Petrified, he stood rooted to the spot, gawking at the demon in front of him. "Demon", the word sounded foreign, and yet so right to him. He didn't know how he knew what to call the monster in front of him.

Piercing golden eyes landed on his eye from through the peephole. A lump lodged in his throat, Del's heart threatened to rupture as the demon approached the door. Footsteps creaked the stale, wooden floor. Eyes wide, Del waited for his doom. Abruptly, the sounds vanished. One minute he was freaking out with every groan of the floor, and the next, a stuffy calm had enveloped the hallway. He let out a shaking breath, apparently, he had forgotten to breathe in all the commotion. Just as his taut body began to relax, the door was flung open, sending Del on a collision course with the opposite wall.

Sneering, the skeleton demon let out a taunting laugh. ***"You think you can escape me, fiend? I am the Skeleton King, and I shall ruin anyone who dares to trespass over my property. Alas, I am a merciful king: you shall be allowed to present your side of the story, but it won't do you much good."***

Del's throat had closed up, he was trembling, and no words came out of his pinched mouth. Arching a condescending figurative brow, the Skeleton King plucked Del up from the floor as if he were as light as flour. Heart plummeting, Del struggled to breathe with the mildew smell that cling to his captor. His time had come—he was sure of it.

The last remnants of his bizarre vision disappeared, as the voices grew more animated outside. The position of the moon told him that he had been asleep for a while. While he glanced around, his laid his hand on his clammy forehead; the back of his neck was also covered with sweat. He saw a lush willow tree with its roots laying around him, but not on him. He hadn't realised it at first, but his wooden chains were now gone. Lurching out of the cramped space, he hobbled towards the direction of the sounds. His eyes almost bulged out of his sockets when he caught sight of the arguing creatures. Willow, it seems, was a personification of his name, but he wasn't as large and big as the original willow. The being he was quarrelling with was uncannily similar to the skeleton demon from his reminiscence.

That, and the fact that he was staring at actual demons scared the wits out of him. What in the world was happening? Demons were just supposed to be fictional crap novelists and producers threw at you, right? Before anyone could shout *April Fools'* at him and end this reality, the skeleton spotted him.

"If he's not here, then what's that I spy among your branches? It looks like a human to me." The bone boy— very small, with a green mistiness to his bones—declared haughtily to Willow.

When Willow looked over to where the reed-like, spooky skeleton hand pointed, he was left breathless for a moment. Overwhelmed with ancient feelings, he gazed forlornly at the outstanding creature that scrutinized him and the scene with disbelief, wonder, and suppressed rage. He was a child once again, who didn't quite understand who he was. Willow scuttled in haste towards Del and engulfed him in a tight hug. Startled, Del tried to free himself, but he was bound staunchly in a different type of chains now. Willow's presence was strangely calming, his naturally earthy smell decapitated Del's lingering fear, leaving nothing but a dull ache in its wake. Closing his eyes, Del reveled in the sensation.

Gradually, Willow eased away from Del and walked away to his tree but not before whispering something to Del.

"We shall aid you when you need us, master."

The words, spoken with such open loyalty and sadness bewildered Del, but he had no time to ponder on them. In a split second, the skeleton gripped his upper arm and was harshly dragging Del along with him. Unbidden memories lashed at him as he passed the unknown yet familiar hallways in the manor. He somewhat knew his way about the spacious house because of the galas. However, it felt too familiar to him: as if he had once lived here in another time, another life. Too many untangled visions assaulted him, as he was being pushed into the same room that he had seen in his dream under the willow tree.

The skeleton monster urged him forward with his menacing face. Del was terrified, just as a person should be when he was supposedly about to die. Unexpectedly, courage, sorrow, and happiness were also unwinding inside of him in rapid succession. His feelings were basically a muddled mess. He felt as if whatever he was about to face would free him from his oppressive prison. By coming to face to face with this skeleton demon, he would finally find himself again. The thoughts churning inside him belonged to someone else—after all—he was just human.

The sheer mechanics of the room jolted Del out of his ocean of thoughts. It was larger than it appeared and a little different from before. The musty wooden boards had been upgraded to pale gray cement tiles. The windows lining the wall that faced the front of the house were still painted red, but they had been polished to look new. What really caught his undivided attention was the metallic stag head above the fireplace. It was all metal, with no paint to soften the harsh, reflective surface. Its antlers were poised as a door's handle to another room, while its murderous eyes were capable of petrifying any onlookers.

With calculated steps, the skeleton demon lit the candles adjacent to the walls, poured a ghastly smelling liquid (it might or might not have been stale blood) into a porcelain bowl, and chanted macabre words. Under his incantations, horrid green fumes began filling the air. For Del, it was becoming increasingly hard to breathe and, as the monster's hysterical hissing continued, the more air Del lost. In a matter of minutes, he was panting vigorously for breath. Labouring for air had never been this excruciating and painful. His throat felt as if it was being strangled by some invisible force. Spit gushed out of his mouth, his lips had gone blue, and he was hyperventilating. Del sank to his knees, his eyes had rolled back in his head, and the pain he felt was palpable. Instantaneously, the pain and the hand crushing his throat vanished into thin air. Del gulped in as much air as he could without coughing profusely. He felt weak: his breath wheezing in and out from his raw throat.

"Still haven't dropped dead yet, have you? Well, no matter, I have got a lot of things waiting for you." The skeleton's maniacal chuckling chilled Del to the bones.

Gathering his nerves, Del croaked out: **"Why?"**

"Got something to say, have you. Hmmm, I should at the very least listen to your plead before ending your miserable existence. Spit out what's eating you inside, even as you face death."

"Why are you doing this? I think I deserve to know why I'm being killed." Del's voice rose in bravo and got steadier as he continued.

Bony fingers tucked under his opaque chin, the demon regarded Del with bored interest and brayed at Del.

"It's not your fault that I am targeting you. Today is the holy night, when we present our killings to our King, Zharagus. I need to kill you to complete my one million killings—to be given the opportunity to become the king's left hand. Only then will I have a chance at revenge. In simple words, you're helping me by dying, and I know how much you humans like to help others—so it's a win-win situation for both of us."

At Del's blank expression, the skeleton smiled malevolently, took out a jar of blue fire from the wardrobe, strode towards his target with purposeful steps, and smiled an evilly brutish smile.

He unscrewed the jar without warning, gripped Del by his collar, and drenched him in the blue flames. The human's agonizing screams filled the room, as the smell of burning flesh emanated from the blazing heap on the floor. The puny human's wails and suffering were like music to the demon's ears. He relished them; he rejoiced his victory with every yelp of pain that burst forth from the lowly human's mouth. Vengeance would finally be his.

Del couldn't believe his luck. He had been set on fire, a fire that was stripping away his very life source before his eyes. He hadn't committed any violent crimes like murder: heck he hadn't even been involved in any white-collar crimes, so why was his life ending so brutally? He was a nobody. He was supposed to live a boring life and then die painlessly. The sizzling hot fire was slowly and hellishly killing his essence. He felt his skin peeling away from his body with a prickling sensation: his eyes were getting increasingly hotter in their sockets. In his mind's eyes, he saw himself as a monster—a monster created by a destructive fire—whose only purpose in life was to wreak havoc. Blood spouted out from his mouth, but his exceedingly raw throat wouldn't stop shrieking like a banshee. After a while, as if on reflex, his throat closed up on him, leaving him no outlet to display the torment he felt. Shutting his eyes, Del waited for the inevitable.

On the other side of the manor, three witches, Uluru, Hana, and Nana, sensed the prophesied coming storm approaching. Haphazardly and quickly falling over each other, with their bulging bellies, their smooth green skin, and pair of elongated goat horns in their hair, the three of them bolted in the direction of the growing tumult. Bursting open the previous Skeleton King's private chambers, the witches were greeted with an eerily incongruous sight. Someone was ablaze with the blue flames of hell itself. Baffled by the turn of events, Hana and Nana were openly gaping, trying to put the pieces together. Uluru's incredulous gasp jerked the other two out of their daze.

Fearful, Uluru muttered furiously, **"What have you done? Bonehead! Do you know who you lit up with that fire?"**

"A human?" He had the nerve to sound amused.

Fuelled with rage and terror, Uluru spat out, **"He's the one who killed your precious Skeleton King. He's the true master of the Halloween demons."**

Staring at her as if she were insane, the skeleton demon retaliated.

"Are you in your right mind? He's just a puny human."

His arrogance set off Uluru's fury like oil to flames; she uttered profanity after profanity at his idiocy.

"Now, he'll awaken and curse us all."

Rolling his eyes, he easily blocked the club she had aimed at his skull. His jeering laughter echoed down the hallways, then it was suddenly cut off. A sickle had snapped his head clean off from his vertebrae neck. The sickle was razor-sharp and curved like a crescent moon: it was an abnormality in the weapon-free room he was currently in. His head had rolled over to the far side of the room, so he couldn't actually see his assailant. But he could hear the anarchy being unleased on his body: every single bone of his fleshless body was being snapped into a million pieces. The formidable creature was carrying out the impossible task, no doubt about it—skeleton bones were rigorously flexible—and so ridiculously hard to break. As the glow of his golden eyes disappeared completely, the monster who had managed to do him in turned to face his skull. Striking out a savage kick, he fractured the skeleton's skull into a myriad of pieces: letting the last remnants of his pathetic soul linger for just enough time to comprehend his defeat. Flabbergasted at what he saw, the skeleton's soul was smeared with everlasting shock as it returned to hell.

Returning back to his normal form, Del gazed absently at the chaos and demolition around him. Running his fingers through his raven-black locks, he guessed he might have gone a bit overboard, if the crushed white power around him was any indication. Huffing a sigh, Del paused to give the three witches an unsettling smile. As expected, the smile set their minds churning on the possible consequences. They were probably imagining all the gory ways he could effortlessly employ to eradicate them. He was just teasing them—he really meant no harm to anyone at the moment—except maybe his brother.

The blue flames had torn him apart, found the lingering demon in him, thatched both parts—the human and the demon—together with an unbreakable knot. He now had a demon's strength and unforgiveness and a human's humanly intuition and kindness: a match no demon wanted to ever be faced with. Zharagus was fooling himself if he thought he could get away with sealing him for five hundred years. He would pay like all the others who supported him: Del would feast on them and reclaim what was rightfully his. Then, he would devour the sickening humans.

STORY N. 5: Much Ado about High School

I gazed at the dreary sky; dark, tumultuous clouds lined every inch of it; the sun was gone for its midday routine nap time; as it did every August, entrusting its domain to the clouds. August was also the start of the school year. Usually, I longed for the first of August every summer, but not this year. My father had decided that we would spend the remainder of the year till next winter in our hometown, which was countless miles away from my beloved city. I was being briskly uprooted from the life I had known and loved for the last ten years, and now I was expected to transfer into Woodbridge High, in a town that didn't even have decent Wi-Fi. Being a hormonal teenage girl, I had given my parents grief on their abrupt and obviously wrong decision. They weren't swayed. Instead, my tantrums seemed to have solidified their resolve from iron to steel.

The road trip to the town had been bumpy and just as drab as the weather was. It took us two days to get to town, which outlined mismatched homes, French villas and a close-knit community. Ladies in the street, laden with groceries, pointed at our car as we passed like they had never seen such a car before. Even me, with my disinterest, knew that some folks in town, like the Andersons, were wealthy enough to easily afford expensive cars like a Ferrari F60 America, so it wasn't the car that had the town in such a frenzy. No, it was occupants of the car they were gossiping about. My father had skipped town when I was seven because of his well-paying job in the city. Now, we were back, and as people returning back to this town were a rare sight, tongues were going to wag.

To get to Aunt Grace's house, we needed to cross the main road that ran through the center of the town. This in turn invited more people to poke fun at us, but it was the shortest route, so dad wasn't going to change course anytime soon. After an hour of being on display, like animals in a petting zoo, we finally reached our destination. Aunt Grace was a homely person, who worried about others like a mother hen. She lived in a one-storey house adjacent to ours. For a few weeks, we would stay with her and her family, as we needed to make our house liveable, since it hadn't been occupied for many years. Her cottage was like one out of a fairy tale. It had a straw-like covering on the cemented roof and wood—real wood made up the exterior walls—its earthy smell lingering in the air yards away from the actual premises.

Aunt Grace was waiting for us outside in the dismal weather. She was leaning against the closed door of her house, her shoulder-length, reddish-blond hair was moving with the wind. Waving at us, she sprinted to mom's door, even before dad stopped the car. Wrapping my mother in a hug, Aunt Grace commenced chattering almost immediately. Used to her sister's antics, my mother took her jabbering and helping us with our luggage in stride. Our aunt noticed us when she was done trading rumours with our mother. Squealing, she hugged of all of us: which included me, my sister Kayla, who was fourteen; my sister Catherine, who was nine; and James, our only brother, who was fifteen.

"It's so good to have you all back. The entire family's finally going to be together, after such a long time." With those cheerfully said words, she bustled us into her snug home.

Despite my many protests, we were off to a good start in town. Over the week, before school officially commenced for the year, my parents managed to insert themselves into the circles that mattered. Since my parents had lived here their earlier years, once upon a time, it was not hard to blend in again. However, the same couldn't be said about my siblings, or me for that matter. The four of us were so used to the hustle and bustle of the city, that adjusting to the sereneness of this town was proving to be slightly difficult. When Kayla and James complained to our father, he just shrugged and said to give it more time.

"You'll fall in love with this town when you get to know it a bit better. Stop worrying and think of it as a grand adventure. Trust me, you'll both feel right at home in no time." With one arm flung over Kayla's shoulders and the other over James's, Dad walked them both to their rooms.

The secretive light of dawn penetrated my bedroom windows, nudging me awake with its reddish halo. Staring bleary-eyed at the plaintive scene before me, I saw an iridescent crimson hue splashed onto the indigo sky canvas, with the town slumbering below. No sound broke through the eerie calm that had engulfed the town in the night. In these wee hours of the morning, before the light awakened the sleeping town, I felt as if I were gazing at a reflection. Inexplicably, this town prodded me to dig out its secrets. On the surface, the town looked like any other place with happy people living a merry life, but it seemed overly pretentious to me. There was no reason I should have felt like that, when I hadn't even lived here, yet the feeling of foreboding remained.

Five minutes before eight, my father dropped me, Kayla, James, and Aunt Grace's twin girls, Mallory and Maya, who were about my age, in front of the school buildings. Woodbridge High and Middle Schools were neighboring, while the elementary school was one block away. Dad wished all of us a good day and hit the gas, so that he could reach Catherine's school in time. I was dressed in a rainbow-patterned tee with formfitting navy blue jeans, my straight, dark brown hair hung in waves behind my back, while James was snuggled into a grey hoody matched with dull green pants. The twins were on another whole level than us. In their brightly coloured Sunday dresses, they appeared prepped to go to a party, rather than school. With rainbow-painted nails, the twins stopped us before we could enter the school building, appraised our clothes, gave a condescending harrumph, and left us with puzzling advice.

"You're new here, so don't go poking into someone else's business. Keep to yourself, don't meddle into anyone's affairs, and you'll blend in just fine. But, piss someone off, and your high school life will be made a living hell. Got that, you two? Now get moving." Mallory's urgently uttered words, spoken with such conviction, left both James and I dumbfounded. With furrowed brows, we separated to go find our respective classrooms.

With my mind still churning with muffled thoughts, I found myself standing in front of my new class, drawling out an introduction.

"I'm Clary May. My family moved into town a week ago. It's nice to meet you all."

"Thank you, Clary. You can choose any one of the empty seats." The teacher left the room, but not before directing me to my seat.

The whiteboard said self-study time, so I decided to observe my classmates. They were just like any typical class who had been given freedom from the teacher. Jocks and cheerleaders sat at the rear of the class, immersed in gossip, the brains occupied the front row, and average folks without a label filled the middle. It was your average classroom, equipped with the vast variety of students that could be found in high school. As time passed, the students became progressively rowdier. One boy, in particular, was making a scene. He was tall, with cropped, sandy-blond hair, his confident posture exuding arrogance and wealth. With pointed taunts and jeers, he was continuously scorning the nerds of the class.

"Andie, sweetheart, how do you make your hair grow so bush-like and frizzled? It's uncanny. You look like a freaking cartoon . . ."

He reeled on and on about Andie's, Sam's, Alex's, and other geeks' appearances, or some other trait. This sandy blond-haired boy was a bully: through and through. If I were at my old school, one word from me would have been enough to put him in his place, but I was in uncharted territory. I didn't know how the bullies and other students would react to my interference. Despite my aggravation, watching from the sidelines was my only sensible option—all the others would result in too much heartache—and I'd rather avoid that. While I was woolgathering, the bullies had either decided to level up, or what they were about to do was a norm here.

With a practised ease, he had elongated the knife of a paper cutter and was ambling towards Andie, like a predator circling its prey. A wild look replaced the carnivorous hue of his eyes; he seemed eager, almost frantic, to do whatever he was about to do. His face was alight with delight. I had been so transfixed by his changing expressions that I hadn't noticed when the steel blade sliced the skin of her arms to red ribbons. Rather than stopping, the blood-smeared blade continued to destroy Andie's skin: first her arms, then her neck, followed by her thighs. The metallic scent of blood was filling the air. The stank, coupled with the sickening scene, twisted something inside of me.

Heart thudding out of control, I deucedly glanced from side to side. No one made any attempt to stop him. If this kept on, Andie might seriously end up in the hospital. With feigned confidence, I urged my feet to move. These people, with their indifference, were even more frightening than the cruel bullies. Without a moment's notice, they would heartlessly throw any defender to the wolves, for their own safety. Gulping a few shaky breaths, I darted towards Andie. My sudden movements nonplussed her accuser, who was in the midst of maiming her ears. I stepped in front of the tattered girl, widening out my shoulders, and faced him head on.

His face took on a look of bafflement, which in just a nanosecond changed to outrage, then to malice, mingled with mockery. The lightning speed shift in his countenance made me wonder if he was on narcotics. He seemed unruly and uncontrollable, traits which were quite common among drug addicts.

Smirking, he sneered at me.

"The new kid thinks she's the mighty Thor. Well, honey, it's your first day, so we'll let this stunt go, but interrupt me again, and it won't be Andie on the floor but you." His voice turned from amused to deadly as he delivered his threat.

Turning his back to me and the whole class, he left with an entourage of about ten to twelve other students, who I guessed were probably just as vicious and mean as him. Ignoring the myriad of looks leveled my way, I sank to my knees besides Andie, examined the extent of the damage, and tried making small talk with her to calm her erratic trembling a bit. I was abruptly pushed aside, with a boy wearing an ugly black hoody taking my vacant place. Rubbing Andie's back, he conversed with her, but unlike my attempts, his turned out to bear fruit. Under his steady gaze, Andie was wailing like a child, her tears smudging his hoody, and she was calling his name over and over again, **"Alex. Alex . . ."**

"Shouldn't we, um, take her to the infirmary or a teacher? She's badly injured."

With a shuttered face, Alex rebuffed me, **"Thanks for stopping those jerks, but if you want to stay safe, then stop meddling in other people's affairs."**

Annoyed, I lashed out, my voice dripping with sarcasm. **"Gee, thanks for your sound advice. Next time, I'll let an innocent girl be tortured without interfering, if I must, and let her injuries burden my conscience."**

My words were pointedly disregarded, and some of the other students crouched down to tend to her wounds. Apparently, while I had been focused on Andie and Alex, the other pupils of the class had come to life. It was a hive of activity, with everyone running around to fetch bandages, towels, and medicine. It was strange really; they had been like puppets when the bullies—jocks and other popular kids—were around, but now I could see their true potential. With reassuring hands, a nerdy-looking guy, with round-rimmed glasses, cleaned and covered up Andie's cuts. Wet towels and bandages were constantly being brought in by some of the athletic students. It felt as if I were in an emergency ward, rather than a classroom of twenty-some, seventeen-year-old teenagers, who shouldn't be this efficient, but they were.

The same odious acts were carried out every day, as the days eclipsed into a month. Sometimes on the other geeks, but mostly on poor Andie. It appeared that Sean, the bully with the sandy blond hair, had some hidden grudge against her. I wanted to slap the bully, bang his head in the wall, and hurl insult after insult at him, whenever he hurt Andie and the others. However, Alex, Maya (my cousin), and a few other class fellows had taken in upon themselves to keep me in line. I didn't understand their reluctance: still I had a feeling it had something to do with not making things worse than they already were, even if no one was openly saying it. They were cowards in my opinion. At the moment, I was biggest wuss of them all. I should stick up to my justice-loving spirit and face the bullies with bravery, but every time when Alex and the others peered at me with panic-stricken eyes, I would relent to their hushed pleads. At first, I thought only my class had lunatics, but I later found out that every grade from ten to twelve had some students with macabre tendencies—usually the popular ones.

Irked with the caustic noninvolvement of the teachers, I was heading to my World History class, sometime around noon. It had happened again this morning. This time, the girls had sneaked into the locker room while Andie was showering after a gym class. They had meticulously made all her clothes disappear. She had been left with no choice but to phone me, her voice breaking as she told me what had happened. I'd hoped nothing dreadful would occur before I reached the locker room. Alas, I was proven wrong, yet again. They had humiliated her in the worst possible way; the black-hearted girls had brought many students, mostly boys, in front of the locker room and had wrenched Andie outside without a stitch of clothing on her. Racing forward, I wrapped her in my cashmere sweater, whose hem reached her knees. I had never been so grateful to be tall than at that moment. Handing her over to Alex, I stormed into the staff room to file a complaint against the bullies. The teachers were anything but helpful.

"So, what, Miss May? It was an accident. Andie Hugh misplaced her clothes, so a huge spectacle resulted. I know the students pretty well, and it's my opinion that Miss Hugh chose to come out nude for publicity. High school girls are always looking for a chance to insinuate some drama."

These days, I was always seething, ready to explode at any moment. Breathing out an irritated sigh, I rounded a corner, only to come to an abrupt halt. Eyes wide, I retreated backwards until I was hidden behind the wall, and peeped at the Sean and his two friends superstitiously. Their feral smiles hinted that they were up to no good. Straining my ears, I was able to catch snippets of their animated conversation.

"You're right. We need to do something worthwhile; it's gotten so boring here."

"Sean, why don't we play a little with Andie Hugh? It'll be fun."

"Jason is right. We'll have so much fun tormenting her." His two pals agreed.

His smile widened and turned even more wild as he considered the appalling idea.

"Why not? We'll gang rape her and then leave her in some garbage dump. Besides, no one would to say anything to us, even if the truth got out."

Hearing those words, the walls closed in on me, my head was spinning, and I was having trouble breathing. Rubbing the heel of my palm on my aching chest, I skipped class to find Andie and Alex. When I told them of the bullies' scheme, Alex was clenching and unclenching his fists in anger, while Andie was stupefied. Understanding that we needed a premeditated course of action to counter Sean's plan, Alex and I got down to business. During our heated debate, Andie was in a troublesome daze, looking ashen, as if she had seen a ghost.

Flagged on both sides with Alex and I, Andie walked absentmindedly to the parking lot. Near Andie's car, Sean and his two henchmen stood, intently peering at her slow, faltering approach.

"We've got business with Andie Hugh. The two of you can go now. We'll make sure she gets home safe and sound." He raised a dismissing hand at me and Alex.

Catching onto their ploy, we shoved Andie behind our backs and stared daggers at Sean and his crew. When he tried to reassure us, I cut him off.

"We know exactly what you have planned for Andie, and we're not about to let you take her from us."

Narrowing his eyes, Sean glared at me.

"Whatever you're probably thinking isn't compared to what we've planned for Ands here. She will have fun with us; I'm sure of it." He leered at Andie while uttering the last sentence.

"You will have to go through me to get to her." My headstrongness made its appearance, even as Alex's eyes were begging me to rethink my already-on-flames plan.

"Hmm."

Sean's eyes had turned dark. With a shrewd nod at his cronies, Sean grasped my arm and yanked me towards him. Pinning my hands behind my back, he held me against his chest, my back to him. Alex rushed towards Sean with a punch, but his friends intercepted him. He was horribly beaten to a pulp, his nose was bloodied and broken, and purple bruises circled the skin around his eyes when they were done with him. Giving Andie a rueful look, Sean announced to the world at large.

"I really wanted to play with you, Andie, but Miss May here needs to be taught a lesson."

Dread settle into my bones as he drove me in his car from the parking lot to an abandoned warehouse. I was quaking—blood roared in my ears—and my eyes were wide in trepidation as they tied me to a chair. Shoving a table under my chin, Sean gathered my dark brown hair in his fist and pulled it brutally. Searing pain shot through my head; the roots of my hair were being roughly yanked from my skull. I saw black dots when he finally let go. Chest puffed out, my breaths came out ragged.

Smirking evilly, Jason brought over a tub filled with ghastly smelling red liquid. Sean stared at it and then at me. Then, he grinned like a kid who had just received his Christmas present early. Caressing a lock of my hair, he looked at me with malice lacing his eyes.

"Your sisters have strawberry blond hair, but yours is drab brown. I wonder if it'll turn red if we drench it in pig's blood. Legends say that a pig's blood is one of the best natural paints out there."

Nodding to his pals, he added. **"Time to test the theory."**

Without warning, they dumped the blood on me. Mini streams of scarlet blood trailed down my body, covering me in the nasty, metallic stench. Coughing out blood, I shook my head to clear my eyesight and get the liquid off my face. Mocking laughter pierced the still air: the boys were ridiculing me. What had I gotten myself into? Was I going to make it out alive? As my thoughts were rolling along, Sean took out a slender-looking knife from his pocket. Unbuttoning the top three buttons of my shirt, he laid its tip against my collarbone. Gingerly, he dug the tip in deeper, causing me immense pain, and carved a 'S' against my skin. It was a marker—a proclamation of the torture he was putting me through. Satisfied with his penmanship, he suddenly thrust the knife across my wrists, scarring both of them.

His tranquil face, coupled with the suppressed fury in his hands, told me that he wasn't about to let me go anytime soon. With that realisation, my body went numb. They slapped me multiple times, even banged my head hard on the table, but I didn't notice. I was in a bizarre state of limbo—seeing everything—yet simultaneously not feeling anything. So, this was how my life was going to end, I thought, with a heavy heart. I closed my eyes to invite death; it would be better than this torture.

As I sat there, unaware of anything, my life flashed before my eyes. My family and friends' faces appeared to me, as I kept falling into a fathomless black pit. Like a flash of lightening lighting up the night sky, a warm light enveloped me, pulling me out of the darkness. I slowly opened my eyes and saw that I was in someone's arms on the floor. She was rocking my numb body and rubbing my arms, trying to get my blood circulation going again. Against the haze, I heard only these words, underlined with conviction and warning.

"She's mine; I told you so before. Hurt her again, and you'll have to answer to me."

Sean spluttered, which puzzled me, since it was so unlike him. "B-But Susan, she's too meddlesome."

"I don't care. She's mine—and you'll stay away from her from now on. Hurt her, and you'll be making an enemy out of me. You don't want to do that now, do you?"

I fell deeper into myself, with the name of my rescuer on my cracked lips.

Two days later, I woke up in a hospital bed with tubes poking out of my arms. With my weakened and bruised body, I tried to sit up. A yelp escaped me before I could stop it, and my parents were on me like the hounds of hell in an instant. Kissing my cheeks, my mother kept on petting my wriggly, cropped hair—

another gift left by Sean and his bully friends. Staring mournfully at me, my father engulfed me in a bear hug.

"I'm sorry, sweat pea. Your friends told me what happened. This place hasn't changed on bit: I shouldn't have brought you all here."

"It's okay, Daddy, it's not your fault."

While I was in his arms, I remembered my saviour. She was Susan Johnson, the mayor's daughter. Astounded at the turn of events, a flicker of clarity began to take root in my brain. Due to some inexplicable reason, she liked me, and I was going to use that to my full advantage. Susan Johnson was one of the most powerful students in our school, so if she was on our side, we may just have a fighting chance against the bullies. Resolving myself, I closed my eyes and nestled into my father's embrace.

STORY N. 6: The Black Cat

Isabelle was running for dear life in those dimly lit hallways, looking back every now and then to check if she was being followed. He would catch up with her soon. She turned a corner to find herself in front of a door. The only door she had been able to find in the entire house. With quivering hands, she repeatedly turned the door's handle, trying to open it somehow or the other. She had to hide, or he would devour her. He had been chasing her for many nights now. Isabelle was a beauty in her own right, but not tempting enough to captivate a stalker. His interest in her mystified her. She needed to escape before he found her—and fast. Rapidly approaching footsteps told her he was gaining in on her, his sawdust smell churning in the night air.

Isabelle was no longer in a locked house, but out in a park. Glancing around frantically, she tried to find a way out of this nightmare. A hooting sound caught her attention during her search. Fear gripped her, and her eyes grew as wide as rounded orbs. He had found her. With feline-like features, he stalked towards her with the elegance of a cat. His perked cat ears were taking in every sound she made, even her shallow breathing. Isabelle blinked once and the next second, he was on her. Claws outstretched, he reached for her. He was finally going to hurt her, like he'd promised before. Terror sank its claws into her before the cat could.

Jerking awake to the sound of her alarm, Isabelle found herself in the real world again. The feral cat had been haunting her dreams for weeks now. The same scenario she saw now, she had witnessed almost all those other nights as well. With her aching body, she got out of bed and dressed for work. Isabelle was a reporter in a local newspaper firm. Stuffing toast into her mouth, she made haste.

As her heels clicked on the pavement, she saw something peculiar out of the corner of her eye, in the crowded street near her workplace. It looked like a woman, who was cowering against something or someone. Something about the woman was calling to her; Isabelle needed to talk to her to ease her thumping heart.

With uncertain steps, she made her way to her. When Isabelle was standing in front of the crouched woman, something strange happened. She gripped Isabelle's hand staunchly and started muttering under her breath. Before her eyes, the woman transformed. Her crouched figure gave way to a hunched form with pearly white skin. With her gangly hands, she twisted her face until it was upside down: the creaking of her neck bones sent shivers down Isabelle's spine. Other than her, no one seemed to have noticed this metamorphosis.

"I told you I'd follow you to the ends of the earth if I have to."

The creature's needling words were followed by an ear-spitting sound in the air. In a wink of an eye, Isabelle was no longer on the road, but in that same house of her nightmares. Belatedly, she realised she had been dreaming all along. She desperately tried to wake up, but to no avail. This time, the cat spirit was in control and he wouldn't let go of her so easily. Trapped and feeling terrified, Isabelle screamed: her throat raw in frustration and fear.

Feeling a hand on her shoulder, Isabelle saw that the black cat from her nightmares was draped over it. In a jiffy, it was replaced with the cat demon. The cat demon's sharp, yellowish claws were poised at her throat, his tail wagging in anticipation.

Smiling intimidatingly at her, he whispered in her ear.

"Good-bye for now. See you soon." With a contended purr, he strode away.

With the image of his retreating back, Isabelle's eyes popped open to gaze at her boss, who was looking at her with annoyance. He often caught her sleeping in the office, a result of her troubling dreams. The whole week, she dedicated herself to find a way to stop her nightmares. Her discoveries were varied, but most of them weren't accessible to her in the city she lived. Shoulders sinking, she gave up on finding any possible way to get rid of the demon that had latched itself onto her.

A month later, when his antics drove her to almost drown herself, she sprinted to the nearest church she could find. The pews were empty of people, with only the priest present. He took in her bed-ragged clothes, the dark bags under her eyes, and the overwrought expression on her face, and invited her to pray her woes away. Murmuring to God, she followed the priest's advice, but it didn't help ease the discomfort that had residing in her since the dreams had started.

She decided to take her case to the priest directly. With heavy steps, she reached his office and knocked. Just as she was about to lay herself bare to him, gruesome visions peeked out from his aura. The cat demon was showing her what would happen to the priest if she continued. A knife to the gut, a lion circling him mercilessly, a heavy vase falling on top of his head and rendering him brain dead, and many other ghastly visions assailed her. Placing a shuddering hand over her taut throat, she apologized to the priest for wasting his time and then rushed out of the church as quickly as humanly possible.

"Why?"

"Are you speaking to me, little girl?" The black cat demon asked mockingly.

Isabelle all but bellowed in exasperation. **"Yes, you. Why are you haunting me? What did I ever do to you?"**

She would never have ventured to stand up to the demon: he scared her too much for her to do that. However, he had turned her life upside down—too much for her to back down now. She was jobless, friendless, and just short of being declared insane by her family. Her family would often find her talking to herself in a hurried and seething tone.

Smirking blithesomely, he let out a meow.

"You fascinate me with your unwillingness to believe in superstitious facts: like crossing paths with a black cat brings you bad luck. Besides, you fed me, and I'm returning the favour."

Flabbergasted, Isabelle stared at him. **"You're that stray black cat I fed milk to months ago?"**

"That's right."

"Then, shouldn't you be looking out for me, instead of haunting me."

"You opened Pandora's Box when you fed me, which means I shall stay with you for the rest of your life."

And he did. He had stayed with her when her parents admitted her to a mental asylum and also when she would claw her cheeks with her ridiculously long nails. He fulfilled his promise: until she died at the age of seventy-eight years old. The demon who deranged her was therefore her constant companion in life.

CONCLUSION

thank you for buying and reading this book!

if you liked it, I ask you please if you can post a review on the amazon page of this book.

Printed in Great Britain
by Amazon

15873032R00088